Items should be returned on or before the last date shown below. Items not already requested by other borrowers may be renewed in person, in writing or by telephone. To renew, please quote the number on the barcode label. To renew online a PIN is required. This can be requested at your local library.
Renew online @ **www.dublincitypubliclibraries.ie**
Fines charged for overdue items will include postage incurred in recovery. Damage to or loss of items will be charged to the borrower.

Leabharlanna Poiblí Chathair Bhaile Átha Cliath
Dublin City Public Libraries

Comhairle Cathrach
Bhaile Átha Cliath
Dublin City Council

Brainse Ráth Maonais
Rathmines Branch
Fón / Tel: 4973539

Date Due	Date Due	Date Due

D1348757

THE IMAGE
INTERPRETER

Zoran Živković

The Image Interpreter
Copyright © 2016 by Zoran Živković

FG-RS0025L
ISBN: 978-4-908793-39-4

Cover: Youchan Ito, Togoru Art Works

Neoclassic Fleurons font used with permission of
Paulo W–Intellecta Design

Cadmus Press
cadmusmedia.org

THE IMAGE
INTERPRETER

Zoran Živković

Translated from the Serbian
by
Randall A. Major

Cadmus Press
2017

To Edward Lipsett
A great publisher, a dear friend, a good man

Contents

1. Clamor

Mr. Anatole Mirouille—whom you see in the picture—noticed the camera on the seat opposite his own when he looked over the top of his book.

Mr. Mirouille was headed no place in particular on the metro. Soon after retiring two and a half months before, he had started coming down into the metro regularly in order to read. Earlier, he had had neither the time nor the desire to read, but now he could think of no better way to pass the abundance of free time.

Of course, he could have read at home just as well, for no one would have bothered him—he lived alone—but he was surprised to find that the absolute quiet that reigned there got on his nerves. Many people would have found the conditions perfect for reading, but in the dead silence of the little apartment, Mr. Mirouille's thoughts quickly began to wander, preventing him from focusing on the text. He tried to battle the silence with various kinds of music, but even when he turned the volume on the stereo right up it was to no avail.

Mr. Mirouille finally figured out what the problem was. He had worked his whole life in the midst of clamor. He was surrounded by people whose job it was to make telephone calls. Only in the very early days had this caused him any annoyance. Not only had he quickly gotten used to the background noise, but now he could no longer do without it. On those rare occasions over the weekend or during the holidays when he was on duty alone in the large open plan office, he wouldn't be even half as effective as when it was filled with a multitude of his chattering colleagues.

Now he was retired it would be ideal, therefore, to find similar surroundings, in which he would no longer have difficulty concentrating on his reading. He was sure it would be easy. Are there so few places where one can hear people babbling? In cafés, for example. There are always customers talking, and what's more they are comfortable and pleasant—cool in summer, warm in winter. He started visiting a nearby café, and in those first days it seemed to be all he could wish for. He would order coffee, sit at a table in the corner, and delve into a book without the slightest problem, as the lovely chitter-chatter reached his ears.

He became aware of the snag after about a week. The owner's face lost its early warmth. Scowling, he would bring over the coffee, and utter an icy goodbye when he left. Mr. Mirouille didn't need to search long for the cause of these changes. He would sit alone at the table for eight hours, paying for just one cup of coffee the whole time. It was simply bad business for the café owner.

All right, no worries: he would order more coffee. How much was appropriate for eight hours' occupation of a table? Eight cups, perhaps—one every hour? But what was he to do with eight cups of coffee? Even just one was more than enough, especially with his high blood pressure. If he left them there without drinking them, it would make the owner feel uneasy. The other customers would conclude that Mr. Mirouille was staging a protest because the coffee at the café was bad.

He could, in fact, order something else, but what? Alcohol wasn't an option because he didn't drink at all, and eight of anything else would make him nauseous because of his sensitive stomach. So it was that, seeing no other solution, he stopped going to the café and started looking for a new place to read.

However, he had no luck. It turned out that whatever he thought of, just like the café, had some sort of hidden flaw. He spent several pleasant afternoons reading in the waiting room of the train station, only, as the one passenger who never caught a train anywhere, to attract the attention of the security guards. He tried to explain why he was coming there, but they didn't seem convinced, and rather rudely noted down his personal information, threatening that he would end up in the police station if they ever found him there again.

At the zoo, his plans were ruined by the rain. He had no hesitation whatsoever in taking up a place on a bench next to the large monkey cage, where there were always visitors. The guards paid no attention to him because he wasn't disturbing the animals, and he ignored the occasional deprecating glances especially from mothers with children, who most certainly thought that the elderly man holding a book and dressed in an overcoat was some sort of pervert. Under an umbrella, he would seem even more suspicious to them, but that wasn't what prevented him from coming. He stopped simply because when it's raining there are practically no visitors to the zoo, and therefore no chit-chat either.

Before he finally found the perfect place to read, he made one last hopeless attempt: he wrote to the company where he had worked for four decades. Appealing precisely to the longevity of that career, he requested permission to continue coming into his former office.

He wouldn't bother anyone in the least with his presence. He would take up an inobtrusive place in a corner and just read, never saying a word. All he needed was a normal chair, and he would be satisfied with the right to go just once to the toilet. It hurt him a little, though it didn't surprise him, when they didn't even reply.

The idea of reading on the metro came to him one day when he was riding it home. With surprise he noted something that had been right in front of him all those years, which he had been too blind to see. Almost half the travelers in the metro pass the time reading. He would undoubtedly have noticed sooner if only he had himself read while riding the metro, instead of mainly just staring blankly ahead of himself. People notice only what they are interested in. He had read somewhere that pregnant women have the impression that the world has suddenly filled up with pregnant women.

Of course! He wanted to cry out for joy. The metro had everything he was looking for. Above all, no one reading there aroused any kind of suspicion. In addition, he wasn't exposed to the elements. Like in cafés, in the carriages of the metro it was comfortable and climate controlled, he could sit as long as he wished, and no one would scold him for not ordering enough. Finally, as a retiree, he had benefits, so he could ride all day long for a pittance.

Five times a week, from Monday to Friday, he spent six hours reading in the metro. He would get on as soon as the morning rush had passed, and get off just before the start of the evening one. He avoided the busy times because the clamor then was louder than he liked, and it wasn't easy to find a seat free. Between the two crowded periods, while the cars were half-full, the voices in the background quite suited him. He devoured book after book, almost unaware of the people around him.

On this day, he scolded himself for not paying at least a little attention to his immediate surroundings. All three places around him were, in fact, empty at the moment, but if he had just looked up once in the past few minutes, he would have noticed who had last sat opposite. That person must have forgotten the camera on the seat.

Perhaps they had not yet left the car. He got up quickly, picking up the device, and had started to raise it in the air in order to ask aloud to whom it belonged, when he realized that this would be unwise. Anyone might respond, and how could Mr. Mirouille establish whether the person really was the owner? Could he ask for some sort of proof of ownership? Who in the world carried documents like that around with them?

Then it crossed his mind that only the owner would know the brand of the small apparatus. He closed it up in his hand and again began to raise it, but his movements were once again thwarted. They had just arrived at a station. Those preparing to get off did so quickly, and new passengers got on in their places. The opportunity was lost.

Mr. Mirouille was left standing confused, not knowing what to do. He could not, of course, put the camera back on the seat and return to his reading, pretending that none of this was any of his business. If someone came to sit there and simply slid the camera into their pocket, Mr. Mirouille might potentially be accused of being an accomplice to theft, or even of not stopping the theft, when he could and should have done so. Cameras were recording everything in the carriage;

surely he had been filmed picking the apparatus up off the seat.

He sighed. There was no choice—he would have to take it to the lost-and-found office. He wondered what he should do with it until he got there and concluded that it would be best to keep it in his hand. If he were to put it in his pocket, who would ever believe that he did not intend to take it? He sat down again, put the book in his lap, and looked at the station map above the window opposite. Such offices were not located at every station, only at the largest, and the nearest of those was still six stops away.

Two stops passed before he finally decided to do something that had crossed his mind while he was about to sit down. He had refrained, because he felt it to be an unacceptable act of indiscretion. Ultimately, he convinced himself that it was acceptable after all. In any case, they would do the same thing at the office— they would look at the pictures because that was the most reliable way of identifying the owner. The camera's brand could somehow be guessed, but this was in no way true of the photographs taken. If someone were to ask Mr. Mirouille for the camera before he turned it in to the office, in this way he could establish beyond a doubt whether the person was a fraud or the real owner.

Digital cameras are all very much alike, so he easily figured out how to view the photos on the little screen on the back. The first photo was blurry for a moment, then it sharpened.

Mr. Mirouille was unpleasantly surprised to see himself reading. He looked so immersed in the book, it was no wonder at all that he hadn't noticed someone taking his picture from a nearby seat. He hadn't even heard a click, but that could be because they had started making cameras with a silent mode. They were coming up with innovations all the time. Whatever the case, this was certainly inappropriate. People should not have their pictures taken without their knowledge and approval. There must be some article in the law prohibiting it.

He would register a complaint at the lost-and-found office. He would demand that this photograph be erased, and that the owner be chastised if they ever came to collect the thing they had so carelessly lost. If nothing else, they should feel guilty at how they had treated the honest finder who had been willing to make the effort of taking their camera to the office. Not everyone would be so honest, in spite of the video surveillance in the metro.

Then it occurred to him that this could all be done more simply. Why should he bother explaining things at the office, when he could just erase the picture himself? At least that was easily done. He poked at the small buttons around the screen until he established how to go about it.

Once it had happened that, wishing to erase just one photo from his own camera, he had accidentally erased them all. For an instant, he thought that in this case such a mistake would actually be a fitting form of revenge on the impertinent photographer, but then he grew ashamed. Vengefulness did not come naturally to him.

After all, it could actually be that the person meant no harm when they had photographed him. It was probably a harmless tourist who could not resist immortalizing the scene of an elderly gentleman preoccupied with his reading, as if he were in a library of sorts, and not on the metro. True enough, the stranger didn't have the right to do it, and therefore Mr. Mirouille would erase that picture, but he would leave the rest unharmed.

He checked the erasing procedure once more, then pressed two tiny buttons. The photo shrank to a dot in the middle of the little screen which briefly darkened before the next photo appeared.

This time, Mr. Mirouille did not have time to feel anger because confusion got the upper hand. The cause of his perplexity was not so much his renewed appearance on the little screen, as his realization that this photograph had been taken not today, but yesterday. Or last Thursday. Or any Thursday since it had gotten cold, about a month ago, and he had begun wearing sweaters.

He considered going into the metro to read to be no less serious a business than going to work. He paid careful attention to his attire. What he was wearing now was, indeed, less formal, but no less consistent. Once he had had a special color tie for each working day of the week, while now the color of his sweaters was regulated. Today, Friday, he was wearing a red one, while on Thursdays he always wore a green one, as confirmed by the photograph he was staring at.

A swarm of thoughts buzzed in his head, but there was no opportunity for him to focus on one of them because the image changed at that very moment, even though he had touched nothing. He looked at himself again, this time in a blue sweater. So, Wednesday, he just had time to realize, before another change occurred: the blue became yellow, which always came on Tuesday. The only thing missing was. . . However, nothing was missing. Yellow remained for just an instant, making way for the last, brown, which came on Mondays.

Someone has been taking pictures of me all week, Mr. Mirouille concluded in disbelief. The swarm began buzzing again, but it was muffled once more by a series of pictures on the little screen. The cycle began anew, a little faster than before. The photos remained for hardly a second, creating a short-lived palette—red, green, blue, yellow, brown.

With the small part of his consciousness that was not mesmerised, Mr. Mirouille wondered if he should try somehow to stop this slideshow, even if it meant throwing down the camera which was acting of its own accord. He decided instead to remain patient. This couldn't go on for long. If some sort of psychopath had spied on him and photographed him once each day since he had started reading in the metro, then there would be some sixty photos altogether. At this rate of change, it wouldn't last longer than a minute.

Thirty seconds later, the sweaters disappeared. In the pictures it was now September, when it was still warm, so he had gone down to the metro in lighter clothing. Here as well, he could differentiate the days by the clothes he was wearing. Each one had its own color of shirt, or rather its own nuance between snow-white on Mondays and battleship gray on Fridays.

What will happen when the shirts also give out, Mr. Mirouille thought, when it reaches the end, the first day I spent reading in the metro? However, there was no end. The slide show went on, and the viewer tilted his head slightly in order to discern a detail that had appeared in the lower right-hand corner. At first he thought they were letters, but when he held the camera closer he realized they were numbers.

The four-digit number was reduced by one each time the picture changed. Several photos had passed before Mr. Mirouille realized that years were in question, that each new photo was a year older than the previous one. He had missed which year had started this countdown, but it wasn't hard to figure it out. The first year had to be this one, in fact, when he'd brought his working life to an end.

He turned his attention then from the numbers to the pictures. Judging from his clothing, the impossible photographer had always taken his picture either in late spring or early autumn, while the crowds in the metro told him that it was always either when he was headed for work or when he was returning home from it. He looked carefully at his face. With this swift return into the past, his rejuvenation seemed like some sort of special effect in a movie. His hairline moved toward his forehead and his hair grew thicker, the wrinkles were ironed out, his eyes were ever less sunken, his cheeks became rounder and his sagging neck melted away.

While this enchantment lasted, he managed somehow to hush the swarm rushing around in his head. The stingers stabbed him painfully, but in his enthrallment, he withstood it. When the last picture disappeared, however, the fortieth yearly image, ending a remarkable show lasting less than two minutes, the questions could no longer be avoided. Yet all of them were unimportant except for one.

It was actually of no consequence who had taken all these photos, how or why. He didn't really want to know. Only one dilemma bothered him. The photos from the last two months were of him, there was no doubt, but what about those from the previous four decades? In those it was also him, true enough, but at the same time it wasn't. It wasn't, because he remembered quite well that over that long period of time he had never read a single line in the metro, while the man with his ever younger countenance in the forty photos was completely absorbed in reading, as if that were the most important thing in the world—in spite of the crowds, in spite of the fact that he was usually standing, in spite of the clamor that must have been too loud.

Not knowing what else to do, Mr. Mirouille tried to turn the camera back on to watch the slide show once more. The tiny device, however, did not come alive again, as if its batteries had been drained. He fiddled with it for a few moments, then, shrugging, laid it in his lap next to his book.

Looking down the length of the carriage, he was not surprised to find it empty, even though the terminal station was still far away. It didn't matter that no one was there, it was only important that a light clamor was heard. Just the way he liked it. He picked up his book and opened it at the place where he had briefly stopped reading.

2. "Le Boulevard"

Miss Marie-Louise Ponthieux—here she is in the picture—realized that she had forgotten her camera in the metro only once she was a good three hundred yards from the station.

She reached "Le Boulevard" café, which she wanted to photograph, and she was quite happy when she saw that it was still there. The surroundings looked completely different than she remembered—changed, new, modern—but the café was almost the same as when she was last here, July 19th, 1958. In fact, she didn't have to rely on her memory. In her bag, she had a photograph taken at this very spot, right by the door.

Albert had asked a passerby to take their picture, and afterward they had both giggled about how taken aback the man was. It was as if the gray-haired man had never held a camera before. He took the old-fashioned Kodak in his hands almost reverently. Albert tried to calm him down, explaining that everything was set, he just had to push the button, but he couldn't do it, he froze up, his forehead was beaded with sweat, and not just from the heat. Once he had finally pushed the button, an audible sigh escaped him.

Miss Ponthieux now realized that she had had no right to giggle back then. She herself had been nervous when she recently bought a digital camera for her first visit to Paris in fifty-eight years. She didn't actually want one of those, rather one from her youth, with film, but they told her it wasn't easy to find them, hardly anyone used them anymore apart from a few professional photographers, and they were also significantly more expensive.

Though brief, the directions for using it were full of technical phrases she didn't really understand, and she had had to go back to the camera shop where she bought it—one of only two in Langeais—and ask them to explain how to use the gadget in the simplest possible terms. She was interested in nothing more than the most common tourist photographs. She accepted the smile on the face of the helpful young salesgirl as the true price she had to pay for her giggle some six decades before. Miss Ponthieux was not, in truth, in the habit of ridiculing people, quite to the contrary, but that day long ago she had been so joyful that even little things made her laugh.

Now, standing in front of the café, she continued digging through her purse excitedly, even though it was immediately clear that the camera wasn't there. Her fingers usually found it with ease. It irritated her that, every time she wanted to take a picture of something, she had to take it out of her purse, then put it back in, but she couldn't find another solution. She would never even think of wearing it on a strap around her neck like tourists did, although she did have to admit that it was more practical.

Her first thought was that someone had stolen her camera. Before leaving Langeais, several people had told her to watch out for pickpockets in Paris. Next to tourists, their favorite victims were the elderly. She had bought a new bag for that reason, one that was not so easy to open. This had hindered her even more as she kept taking the camera out and putting it back, but she just had to put up with it. With trembling fingers, she started checking whether anything else was missing. If they had also gotten her money and documents, that would be really, really bad.

She let out a sigh of relief when she realized that everything else was still in her bag. She hugged it to her chest. She remained like that for a few moments until she had calmed down. It seemed that no one had robbed her after all, she concluded, and not just because her money and documents were still there. What kind of thief would steal just a cheap camera, and then mess about with closing the purse again? No, there must be some other explanation. And then she figured it out. She had left the camera in the metro.

She blamed the old man in the loud red sweater for everything. She had sat across from him not just because there was an empty seat—there were other empty seats around—but because she thought she recognized him. It was as if she had already seen him somewhere. There was nothing strange about her inability to remember who he might be. For a while now, her memory had been betraying her. She would be unable to recognize a person, even though she was certain that he or she was not a stranger.

If this had happened in Langeais, she wouldn't have cared too much. She would remember who he was the next time she ran into him. It was a small town, people saw each other often, but in Paris it was altogether another matter. If she didn't find out who the gentlemen across from her was, she wouldn't get a second chance. Yes, but how could she find out? She could not, of course, interrupt his reading and inquire about where she knew him from. What would he think of her? Not just that she was imposing, but that she probably had nefarious intentions.

If he would just look up at her he might recognize her, provided, of course, that she wasn't wrong and they didn't know each other at all. However, it was as if nothing in the world existed for him except his book. She cleared her throat to attract his attention, but he remained intently submerged in his reading.

Suddenly, she had an idea. She would take his picture. That should rouse him from his reverie. If he complained about her rudeness, she would pretend that she was taking a picture of the carriage and not of him, and that he was accidentally a part of the composition. If the click of the camera also failed to distract him from his reading, at least she would have his picture, and later she could try to remember who it was that she had run into in the metro.

She removed the camera from her purse and prepared to take the picture. Although she had already taken a dozen or so pictures since arriving in Paris, she was still quite inexperienced, so she had to remember all the things she was supposed to do. After raising the camera to eye level, for a full three minutes she pretended to compose the picture, thus giving the gentleman in the red sweater a chance to notice her, but nothing, it seemed, could distract him from his book.

Taking a breath, she finally snapped the picture. What could be done? She was not destined to find out on the spot whom it was she had met. Just as she turned off the camera, her phone rang in her bag. She'd had a cell phone for years, but she rarely used it. She disliked it, in fact, just like all the other novelties brought about by the new age, but several times it had come in handy that she'd had the telephone with her.

She had brought it along to Paris only because her friend Yvonne had insisted. She had scared her the most about the dangers which lurked on her two-day journey. Pickpockets were the least of the hazards. Yvonne was always afraid of something, and lately she was most worried about terrorists. She was convinced that, once they had taken care of Paris, they would then attack Langeais, where she would be first on their hit-list. She had tried everything to convince Marie-Louise not to visit Paris—she even came up with a story that she had dreamt of someone who looked like her being killed by a collapsing Eiffel Tower. Since she wasn't able to convince her not to go, she insisted that Marie-Louise at least take her cell phone with her so that she could immediately report in if something happened.

Yvonne, however, did not have the patience to wait for Marie-Louise's call, so she had already called twice that morning. Miss Ponthieux guessed it was her again—who else, after all, could it be?—but she couldn't just wilfully ignore the call. She couldn't let it go on ringing in her bag because it would never stop. It would seem strange to the other passengers in the metro that she didn't answer. Perhaps the only exception would be the man reading across from her, because apparently he noticed nothing around himself.

She became confused. She couldn't take the cell phone out with one hand, so she put the camera on the seat next to her. While she opened her bag and fumbled through it, it seemed to her that the ringing was getting louder and louder.

"Hello?" she finally said with a hint of anger in her voice.

"Why didn't you pick up right away?" Yvonne asked without introduction, worried.

"Because my phone was in my bag. I already told you. It's not easy to take it out."

"Where are you right now?"

"In the metro."

A brief silence ensued.

"What are you doing in the metro?"

"Riding it."

"Have you lost your mind?" Yvonne was practically shouting. "Get out of there! Now!"

"Why?"

"How can you even ask! That's the first place they will attack."

"Who?"

"The terrorists, of course! Who else? They choose precisely crowded places like that so that there will be as many victims as possible."

"Calm down, Yvonne, please. It's not very crowded, and there aren't any terrorists. Everything is quite normal."

"It just looks that way to you. . . ."

Yvonne went on talking, but Marie-Louise held the phone away from her ear and stopped listening to her. All at once she became aware of the silence that surrounded her. She turned and saw that everyone who could hear her conversation was looking at her inquisitively—except the man closest to her whom even the mention of terrorists could not distract from his reading.

Oh, Lord, Miss Ponthieux thought. This was all she needed. She had to get out of the carriage immediately. Someone might even call the police.

With her free hand she quickly picked up her bag

and stood up, then headed for the doors feeling the suspicious stares following her.

"Yvonne," she interrupted her friend's tirade, putting the phone back to her ear. "I have to go now. I'll call you later."

"Did something happen? Has the attack started?"

"No, no. Everything is fine. My station is coming up. We'll talk later."

She hung up, even though Yvonne was talking again. She turned the phone off before putting it back in her bag. This would certainly frighten her friend. She would surely rush to turn on her television, convinced that a terrorist attack had started in the Paris metro. When she realized after fifteen minutes that nothing remarkable was going on, she would grow angry at Marie-Louise for not being available, but what could she do? She could no longer allow herself to get into such trouble because of Yvonne's panic attacks.

Stepping onto the platform, she had to force herself to head for the exit without hurrying. Not even turning back toward the windows of the car, she knew that curious eyes were still observing her. She stopped only when the train had pulled out of the station. What should I do now, she asked herself. She had intended to exit at the next station, not this one. She could wait for the next train, but she didn't feel like getting back on. No, she would exit here. It didn't matter that she would have to walk a little farther. Although chilly, it was a nice day, and she would enjoy the stroll.

About twenty minutes later, standing in front of "Le Boulevard" after realizing that her camera was not stolen but that she had left it in the metro car on the seat across from that strange fellow who was reading so ardently—why had it seemed to her that she knew him from somewhere?—Miss Ponthieux again asked herself what she should do. She easily got over the cheap camera, but the pictures she had taken that morning were important to her. And she wanted to take some more. She still hadn't finished.

She thought about it for a moment and concluded that she had to try and find the camera, although that would cost her a lot of time, and afterward she would have to do everything in a rush. First of all, she would have to figure out where the lost-and-found was in the metro. She might be able to find out over the phone, but if she turned it on, Yvonne would realize it immediately and then swamp her with calls. No, she would go back to the metro. She didn't have to walk all the way back to the station where she had exited, there was one nearby.

The station was a small one; there was no ticket window where she could ask, only vending machines. She looked about briefly, expecting to see a member of the metro personnel, but none were around, not even any policemen. She could have stopped one of the few passengers, but they all seemed to be in a hurry, and she didn't really feel comfortable talking to strangers. No choice: she would have to go to one of the larger stations.

Though there were plenty of seats in the car, she decided to remain standing by the rear door. That way she would be as unobtrusive as possible. Her head bowed, she held tightly to the pole with one hand. A full half hour had passed since the unpleasant episode; nevertheless it still seemed that she could sense suspicious looks from the other passengers. She was the first to get off when the train arrived at a major station.

The place was quite crowded, so she lost six or seven minutes before finding the information desk. Then she stood at least as long again in line, though ahead of her there were just a couple of Japanese tourists. They spread a large map of Paris in front of the short, plump, dark-skinned clerk who was explaining something to them patiently in English, to which they simply nodded and grinned, from time to time exchanging short bursts in Japanese. When she did finally get to approach the woman, she learned that the lost-and-found office was just twenty feet or so away from her. She would certainly have noticed if she had just looked in that direction while waiting. Feeling embarrassed, she went over to it.

This time she didn't have to wait. The young agent with tousled hair, a sparse beard and round steel-rimmed glasses, looked up from the computer screen in front of him and smiled.

"Hello," he said, half-questioning.

"Hello," Miss Ponthieux replied. "You see. . . I . . . well. . ." Suddenly she grew confused, not knowing where to begin. The embarrassment she had just managed to suppress overcame her once again. She could have thought through what she was going to say, if not earlier then just moments before while standing in front of the information desk, instead of eavesdropping on the conversation of that ridiculous tourist couple, though she spoke neither English nor Japanese.

"Did you lose something?" the clerk attempted to help her.

"Yes. . . No. . . In fact, I forgot. . . My camera. . . I put it on the seat. . . . Across from the man in the red sweater who just kept reading. . . . Yvonne called me. . . . She always calls at just the wrong moment. . . . She kept talking about terrorists, so I had to leave the train quickly. . . . And so. . ."

Miss Ponthieux fell silent again. Dear Lord, she said to herself, I'm making no sense whatsoever. What will this young man think of me?

The young man waited for several moments, then typed out something on a keyboard.

"You forgot your camera in the metro carriage?"

"Yes, but not just now. . . . Earlier. . . Half an hour ago. . . I didn't even notice that I'd left it. . . . Only when I reached 'Le Boulevard'. . . And then I didn't know where this office was. . . ."

"Which line were you traveling on?"

"The one that leads to 'Le Boulevard'. . . . 'Le Boulevard' café. . . Surely you know of it. . . ."

The young man nodded and then typed out something again.

"What brand is the camera?"

"Brand? I don't know. One of those white ones. . . Silver, in fact. . . They're not very expensive. . . ." Miss Ponthieux suddenly sped up. "But that's not the point. I don't care about the camera. I don't have anything to photograph when I get back to Langeais. Just what I photographed today. . . . That's important. . . . Here. . . In Paris. . ."

"Do you remember what you took pictures of?"

"Of course. Here, I made a list of all the things I needed to take pictures of." She struggled slightly to open her purse, and after digging around briefly she took out a crumpled piece of paper and offered it to the young clerk. "You see how many photos I took, up to 'Le Boulevard'. . . and how many I still have to take. . . ."

He looked over the list, gave the paper back to her, and then typed a little more.

"No one has brought in a camera like the one you

described. Two black ones were found, but that was earlier this morning. One has already been returned to its owner. Somebody will probably bring yours in also, but it's still too early. Finders rarely come here in person. People are busy, they have better things to do. Usually they hand in the stuff they find to some clerk on the metro, and then he brings it in at the end of his shift. If you would leave me your cell phone number, I could call you around five-thirty. By then everything found during the day will have been turned in."

"You don't understand. . . ." Her voice became flustered. "At five-thirty I will already be on the way to Langeais. . . . I can't spend another day in Paris. . . That's impossible."

"No matter, I'd like to get your personal information. We'll send you the camera in the mail if you're unable to come for it. And it might just happen that someone will bring it in earlier, so you might be able to come by once more."

"But if no one brings it in, if they keep it. . ."

"Usually they don't keep things." The young man smiled again. "Not because the world has become more honest, but because of that." He pointed over his head at the small camera that was recording the window at the lost-and-found. "They're all over the metro. It's easy to track down dishonest finders."

Miss Ponthieux sighed. Then she noticed that the young clerk was looking at her inquisitively, his fingers poised above the keyboard, so she dictated to him her name and address and her telephone number. She remained standing there indecisively for a few more moments. If it ended like this, she would feel as if she were leaving without getting the job done, but she didn't know what else to ask, so in the end she too smiled, somehow apologetically, as if justifying herself, and then she headed for the nearest exit.

She had not even reached it before she realized that this thing with the telephone wasn't a good idea. Above all, now she would have to keep it turned on, and Yvonne would keep bothering her. Besides, what if she didn't hear it ringing over the street noise when the young man called? It would be better for him to send her a message. She could check from time to time if it had arrived, and she could call him if she got the message. However, when she turned to go back, someone else was already standing at the window.

She shook her head. She had no time to wait again. She would turn on the phone later, in an hour or two. She would be met by a multitude of Yvonne's missed calls, but if there was one from an unknown number, that could only be the young man from the office. It would be the same as if he had sent her a message.

Satisfied with her own ingenuity, she emerged from the station into the sunny day and began taking a turn around the large square she had come upon, facing for the third time in a short span the difficult question— what was she to do now? It was easier to find the answer this time because, in truth, she had no choice. She would buy a new cheap camera and go on snapping photos. She had to put the time remaining until her return to good use and finish taking the photos on her list.

If she got back the camera she had forgotten in the metro, everything would turn out fine in the end. She even came up with an idea for what to do with the second camera, which she needed even less than the first. She would give it to Yvonne as a present to put her in a good mood. She was sure to be angry at her for turning her phone off, and anyway she had to bring Yvonne something from Paris. At least now she didn't have to think about what to buy her.

Filled with a sudden surge of energy, she headed for the nearest newsstand. She could look for a camera store by herself, they certainly weren't a rarity here, but why waste time? She hadn't the least hesitation in asking the saleswoman at the newsstand. She must be used to having people ask her things in such a crowded place, full of tourists. At least now she wouldn't have to answer in a foreign language.

The middle-aged redhead with heavy glasses was indeed obliging. "Second street to the left," she said brightly, pointing down the boulevard. "Just around the corner. You can't miss it." She paused for a moment and then added, "I don't send tourists there. There are other stores for them. . . ."

When Miss Ponthieux turned into the short, narrow street, it was as if she were back in the suburbs. There were almost no people or cars there, and the noise from the boulevard wasn't as loud. The shop windows were fewer, and they were less flamboyant. If she hadn't been told that the store was just around the corner, she wouldn't have recognized it by the display behind the not-so-clean glass: a vintage bellows camera surrounded by a scattering of black-and-white photos. This, she remembered, is what photo studios used to look like long ago. She looked up, but there was no sign at all. Had the saleswoman at the newsstand perhaps not understood her and sent her to the wrong place?

Stepping inside, she had to linger on the threshold until her eyes grew accustomed to the gloom. Yet, even seeing so little, she realized that this was not the store she was looking for. In the rather small room there were no cameras. All the walls were covered by framed black-and-white photos like the ones in the shop window. To the left, there was a small round table and two massive armchairs, and across from the door was a counter. Behind it stood an elderly man with gray hair and a beard, in a dark suit with wide lapels. His large dark red bowtie matched the handkerchief that peeked from the upper pocket of his jacket.

"I'm sorry, I made a mistake," said Miss Ponthieux, feeling uncomfortable.

"No you didn't," the gentleman responded warmly. "You're in the right place."

He came out from behind the counter and moved forward to greet her. Approaching her, he took her by the fingers of her free hand, bowed and gently touched them with his lips. She didn't realize what he was up to, so she didn't manage to react. No one had kissed her hand now for. . . so many years. She quickly withdrew her hand as he began to straighten up, but was immediately ashamed of her hastiness.

They stood there briefly, close together. She took him in with one swift glance, then lowered her gaze. She was overcome by the same impression that she had had in the metro. Up close like this, the stranger seemed familiar to her, even more than the reading man in the red sweater, but again she couldn't remember who he might be.

"I thought that cameras were sold here. . . . A misunderstanding. . . The woman at the newsstand. . ." She indicated the boulevard. "I left mine in the metro. . . ." Oh, Lord, she thought, here I go rambling again. "I'm sorry. . . . Good bye. . . ."

She turned quickly to leave, but his voice stopped her. "You wish to buy a camera?"

She slowly turned around.

"How did you know?"

"That's all we have here. Special cameras."

"Special?"

"Yes. I'll show you right now. Please, come over here."

He went toward the counter, but she did not follow him.

"No, thank you. I don't need a special one. . . Just a regular one. . . . Later I'm just going to give it away to. . . I'll look in another. . . Good bye. . . ."

She started to leave again.

"Don't you even want to see it? I would say that this is precisely what you need."

She hesitated briefly, this time only turning her head. On the counter in front of the salesman was a vintage camera. She sighed. He was persistently trying to sell her goods she didn't need. However, she was suddenly overcome by misgiving. It was as if she had seen this camera before. Damned memory, she whimpered to herself. Can't you remember anything?

And just then, for the first time that day, her memory took pity on her. The recollection surfaced initially as a sound. Somewhere from inner depths, the laughter of a merry girl echoed out. Just an instant later, she saw the face of the gray-haired man who took forever to snap the shot. Finally, she clearly saw in her mind's eye the camera that Albert had given him, asking him to take their photo in front of "Le Boulevard" café.

She tottered toward the counter. For a while she investigated the camera, and then she looked up at the salesman. She wanted to ask him several questions, but she didn't know how to formulate them. If she started rattling incomplete sentences together again, it would be worse than if she had said nothing.

"Good old Kodak," the gentleman saved her from her troubles. He gently patted the camera. "The film is already loaded, you have nothing to worry about. Black-and-white. That was what you originally wanted, right?"

She was aware that she should repeat her question of a moment ago, "How did you know?"—but instead she just nodded.

"Do you remember how to use it?"

She was proud that she could nod her head again. Other things might slip irretrievably away from her memory, but not that. Yet, at that moment she was saddened by a sudden thought, so she started shaking her head.

"No, I cannot buy it. . . . They explained it to me in Langeais. . . . They're very expensive. . . Only professional photographers. . . I told you, just a regular old. . ."

The salesman smiled. "You don't have to buy it. You can rent it."

"I didn't know you could. . . Renting must be expensive. . . ."

"It's free of charge."

"Free?" she repeated in disbelief. "Then the deposit must be a lot. . . . I. . . Maybe I don't have enough. . ."

The gentleman's smile grew wider. "There is no deposit. No sort of payment. It would cost you nothing. Freely make use of the camera."

Miss Ponthieux squinted for a moment. "Just like that. . .? How can you be sure. . .? I mean, not me, of course. . . I will bring it back. . . . But someone else. . .?"

"Other people don't know about our store. Only trustworthy people come in here."

Although Miss Ponthieux should have been satisfied with the favorable circumstances, two dark clouds immediately appeared in her clear blue sky. It was part of her nature. Ever since the misfortune she had experienced in her youth, she simply could not see herself as one of destiny's favorites. In every good thing that happened to her—and they were rare enough—she would always look for a dark side.

In the first place, if she accepted the kind offer, she would have to wear the bulky camera on a strap around her neck, like the tourists. She wouldn't dare to be separated from it for a moment. She was horrified at the possibility that she might forget this treasured object somewhere, like the other one, the (fortunately cheap) camera she had left in the metro. If something similar were to happen again, her only recourse would be to kill herself. And then, there was still the gift for Yvonne. Without the second camera, she would now have to come up quickly with something to buy her, and waste time shopping. However, time was growing ever shorter.

Again she sighed. "If I had only known earlier about your store. . . Your good faith. . . This morning I already could have. . . Then I surely wouldn't have lost. . . Or the pictures. . ."

"You didn't lose your pictures. Not the ones you took on your way here, or the ones you still have on your list. They are already here." He laid his fingertips on the camera. "Didn't I tell you that it is special?"

This time she kept her eyes fixed on his white smiling face. She restrained herself valiantly from uttering her usual "How do you know?" It wasn't easy to oppose her own nature. In the end, the scale was tipped by a simple realization which she should have had many years ago. She did not have to conjure up the dark clouds; there were more than enough of them to darken her skies without her wishing. After all, are lottery winners troubled by the question of why it is their numbers have been drawn? She had been cordially informed that the camera was special: why ask for any further explanation? Is it important why and how the sky is clear?

"Well, actually not quite all of them," the gentleman finally broke the silence. "There is one more photograph to be taken. 'Le Boulevard' café. You must do that yourself, Miss Ponthieux."

She nodded, and smiled herself for the first time. This did not demand further questioning either—everything was understood. He once again went around the counter and picked the camera up. Before offering it to her, he took her hand once more and put his lips to her fingers. This time, she certainly did not jerk her hand away.

A strange thought crossed Miss Ponthieux's mind after she had left the little store and headed toward the boulevard. If Albert were alive, would he look like this gentleman? He was somewhat taller than him, but people get smaller as they age. He didn't have a beard, but he could have grown one. His voice was different, but voices change over the years. Was her voice the same as when she had come as a young woman with her fiancé to Paris? In any case, she would like it if Albert looked like this man—handsome, well-mannered and well-dressed. And his graying hair looked really good on him.

Passing by the newsstand, she turned toward the shopkeeper. The woman smiled and waved. Miss Ponthieux nodded back, then headed off toward the metro station.

Albert had to go to Paris on business for two days. She was quite happy when he invited her to join him, although she knew that this would be a source of gossip in Langeais. It was not a big town, everyone knew everyone, everyone poked their noses into everyone else's business. But all would be quickly forgotten after the wedding in August. Just because of a little gossip, was she to give up on a chance to see Paris for the first time, even briefly, and with Albert at that?

They were supposed to go by train, but a railway workers' strike was imminent, so at the last moment they decided to go by car. Already on the road she began to laugh about everything, intoxicated by the green landscapes, Albert's tangible proximity and good cheer, by the rushing juices of youth and the promises life gives so generously at the beginning.

The laughter went on in Paris. Albert quickly finished up his work, and then the rest of the day belonged to them alone. She felt no fatigue from the long drive, while her fiancé took her from one place to the next, places she had previously only heard or read about. It seemed to her that she could go on walking forever, that the enchanting city had an inexhaustible store of sights for her wonderstruck eyes.

It was lovely that Albert had brought a camera. These moments should not be allowed simply to pass away; they needed to be preserved, because nothing would brighten the winter grayness of Langeais better than an album full of delightful summertime photographs. And there would be no better memento of how close she had come to happiness when she, like everyone else, was inevitably struck by the things misfortune had planned for her.

Obliging passersby took turns behind the camera, infected by the mirth of the young couple, and they would go away smiling after taking their picture. Everyone except the gray-headed gentleman in front of the "Boulevard" café, who was truly relieved when he gave the camera back to Albert. The man had not gotten far enough away, when Marie-Louise burst out laughing uncontrollably. She would have been ashamed in some other situation, but that day she did not feel remorse for a single one of the sins she committed.

Entering the crowd at the big metro station for the second time, she first looked toward the information booth. She was not surprised when she again saw the Japanese tourist couple with their map spread out, nor when they smiled and waved at her, together with the dark-skinned clerk. The shaggy young clerk at the lost-and-found office did the same. She responded to all of them by raising the hand with the camera.

Entering the metro carriage, she took a seat without hesitation. No one had reason to notice the elderly woman who was hugging her purse with one hand and holding a camera in the other. This invisibility was much more in her veins than her earlier conspicuousness. She had spent the last fifty-eight years completely unnoticed, just like everyone else who withdraws from life.

Though she was gifted with premonitions of misfortune, she had suspected nothing. They stayed late in bed at the little hotel and spent the rest of the morning on a fresh tour of Paris. Then they went to lunch, got in the car and set off for Langeais. Marie-Louise was additionally thrilled by Albert's suggestion that they take the back-roads and enjoy the beautiful countryside covered with castles.

They were driving along a narrow, winding, almost

deserted road through the vineyards, when the automobile suddenly swerved. They were not going fast, so Albert easily regained control. Front left tire, he said, after stopping the car and getting out to check what the problem was. I have to change the tire. Good timing, she replied, and then whispered to him with a little smile, I need to pee. Just the day before she would have hesitated to blurt out anything of the sort to her fiancé, but the intimacy that had meantime been established between them allowed, even demanded, such openness.

Squatting behind a bush, she heard, in short order, the fast approach of a car, sudden braking, a thud, and then someone speeding away. The driver didn't even slow down, much less stop. Several long moments passed until, all in a panic, she managed to finish her business and return. The car had gone fairly far away, so she was unable to discern the letters and numbers on the license plate, and since she knew nothing about cars, she did not recognize the make or model.

Then, trembling, she turned back to Albert's automobile. . .

The small metro station where she got off was as empty as the first time. There was no one there for her to greet, so she hurried out.

Yvonne was astonished when Marie-Louise suddenly told her that she planned to go to Paris for two days, the same length of time as her previous sojourn there. But you haven't been there in—how long? Fifty-eight years. But why now, in November? Marie-Louise did not answer this question, even though Yvonne went on asking it until the day she left. If an anniversary had been in question, Yvonne would have understood her decision, whilst still being opposed to the trip, but she also would have wondered why Marie-Louise had missed so many other anniversaries.

The answer was never given because it was unpleasant, and also because of Yvonne's tendency to panic. How could she have told her, and not scare her to death, that she could not put off the trip for the next upcoming anniversary because she had had a clear premonition that July 19th next year would be too late. She would either go now, or never. And Marie-Louise's premonitions about misfortune had been wrong only once. Completely insulated by her happiness, she had had no premonition of Albert's death.

Arriving once again at "Le Boulevard" café, she did not have to check the photograph in her purse as to where the gentleman had been standing when he took their photo. She remembered the exact place, so she stood there and prepared the camera for the picture. It is so much easier to handle, she thought, than one of those new-fangled digital doodads.

She had to be patient until the crowds thinned out. She did not want anyone to be in the frame. In the original photograph there was no one except her and Albert. When her chance finally came, she quickly brought the camera up to her eye, but she did not snap the photo. Something was wrong. She expected to see the same thing through the little window as she did with her naked eye, but somehow the colors had gotten lost. What she was looking at was black-and-white. Confused, she lowered the camera for a moment. The colors, of course, were still there. When she raised it again, they disappeared, as if she were looking at a photograph already taken.

How is this possible, she wondered? Remaining briefly reflective, she couldn't think of any better explanation
than that this was not that old, everyday Kodak of Albert's, with which something like this would be impossible, but a special camera that should not surprise her
in any way. Who knew why it had to be just like that.

Holding it ready, she waited for an elderly woman
with her little dog to leave the frame. Although dressed
in a modern fashion, in black-and-white she seemed
to be from some older time. She looked at Miss Ponthieux, then smiled at her, probably as a sign of com-
radeship in age. The answering smile remained hidden
behind the large camera.

Marie-Louise finally snapped the shot. She kept
the camera raised for a moment or two, unwilling to
lower it. At once she became aware that this was the
last picture she would take. That, at least, was what
the gentleman from the store had said, and he was to
be believed. All the other items from her list had been
photographed; only "Le Boulevard" café remained.

And now it stood before her, transformed, once she
had lowered the camera. Her surprise would certainly
have been greater if she had not been prepared by what
she saw through the tiny window. While everything
else around was in color, the little café was black-and-
white, just as it would be in the photo she had just
taken and just as it was in the other one, in her purse,
snapped so long ago.

This time she did not even begin to look for an explanation. She merely repeated to herself the conclusion
of moments before, that nothing should surprise her,
and then something else took precedence. She was not
afraid of her rising premonition as she had been earlier
in life, because she knew that it was not a misfortune

that was coming. No, to the contrary, something truly, truly beautiful was about to happen.

At first, the sound had been hardly audible, so she wasn't sure if she was just imagining it. Then the door of "Le Boulevard" café opened, and from inside echoed a resounding, cheerful male laugh. A laugh she would have recognized among countless others. Laughing also, Marie-Louise almost ran inside the black-and-white space before her.

3. Beauty

MR. ALAIN RIGOUD—WHOM YOU see in the picture—had just taken his cell phone from the inside pocket of his black jacket to look at the photographs he had taken twenty minutes or so before, when his attention was caught by an elderly woman who sat down across the aisle in the metro carriage. She was sitting opposite from a likewise elderly man in a bright red sweater who was immersed in reading a book, and she began staring at him.

It seemed to Mr. Rigoud that he had already seen this rather short gray-haired lady, with her round face, old-fashioned dress and bulky black purse. If she would just say something, he could easily establish whether he knew her and from where. He didn't remember faces well, but voices he did. It was enough for him to hear someone once and he would never forget them again. Yet it wasn't likely that the old woman, obviously alone in the metro, would have cause to speak. Unless, of course, it turned out that she recognized the gentleman across from her. She was doing her very best to get his attention—there, she was about to take his picture—but it was of no use because he never took his eyes off his book.

Then the woman's phone rang in her bag. She fumbled about while she set the camera on the seat next to her and took out the phone. She had only to utter two or three words for Mr. Rigoud to be convinced of his mistake. He had never heard that voice before. He instantly lost interest in the old woman and focused on the pictures on his phone. Thus he missed the mention of terrorists, as well as the woman's hurried exit at the next station. He also failed to notice that in the confusion she had left her camera behind.

If someone had been sitting beside him, Mr. Rigoud would have avoided looking at the pictures while still in the metro, even though he was deeply interested in them. There was nothing improper about them, of course, but he was uncomfortable with the idea of someone accidentally seeing them. Who knows what they would have thought of him if they'd discovered that his phone was full of pictures of graves.

Mr. Rigoud had not been to a cemetery for almost forty years: since his father's death. Throughout that time there had of course been reasons to go to funerals, but he'd always managed to avoid them. He had gotten quite skillful at evasion. As soon as he learned that someone had died whose funeral he ought to attend, he would usually leave town and go as far away as possible, even to another continent. That not only justified his absence—could anyone expect him to arrive at a burial from the other side of the planet?—but also gave him the opportunity to visit places he would probably never have seen otherwise.

Illness was also a good excuse, but it didn't have the benefits of travel. For the sake of authenticity—what if someone suspected he was just pretending and then dropped by to see how he was?—he would actually get sick. They were mainly minor infectious diseases—colds, flu, viral or bacterial infections—and only in special cases did he choose something more serious, like mumps, chicken pox or scarlet fever. Doubtless other people might struggle to become infected at will, but not he; he had spent his whole career in the pharmaceuticals industry. Many doctors owed him favors and could hardly wait to return them, never asking too many questions.

His favorite ploy was to have one of his otherwise healthy legs put in a cast. He did not have to break it for real because no one was so skeptical as to ask to see the x-ray. The sole downside was that he could only resort to this trick on rare occasions. He "broke" his leg only twice in forty years, first the left, then the right. Were he to have done it a third time, he would certainly have become suspect, if not as someone who cleverly avoided funerals, then as someone who was a harbinger of them. As soon as Mr. Rigoud showed up with a cast on his leg it would seem like someone was in mortal danger.

When he got the news three days ago that his last school friend had died, Mr. Rigoud began first, unavoidably, to wonder what excuse he would select this time. He did not get far in considering the possibilities available, however, because an unexpected idea crossed his mind. Wouldn't it be better if this time, instead of jetting off somewhere or contracting a disease, he finally went to the funeral?

Although unexpected, the idea did not simply appear out of nowhere. It was instigated by the one question he had tacitly asked himself whenever the obligation arose for him to go to the cemetery. If he did not show up for other people's funerals, what right did he have to expect that anyone would come to his? He had a ready-made answer for this which had always satisfied him until now. It did not matter to him who would come, or whether anyone would come. At his own funeral he would be dead anyway, and thus he would never know who had been present.

That answer, however, was no longer enough, although nothing fundamental had altered. He didn't question whether he would be dead at his own funeral, and therefore unaware of who had come to see him off from this world. The only difference stood in the fact that suddenly it mattered to him.

He did not attempt to fathom the reason for this change of heart. In any case, it didn't seem important. People change as time goes by, this was how he now saw things, and he would act accordingly. So it was that, for the first time in almost forty years, Mr. Rigoud donned the appropriate attire—fortunately, he had a black suit which he used for solemn occasions when protocol required—and headed for the cemetery.

While riding the metro, he recalled his father's funeral for the first time in ages. He remembered it not so much for the sad event—he had not been close to his father—as for the awful weather.

November that year was quite rainy and cold, and on the day of the funeral it was as if the clouds had melded with the earth. It was raining cats and dogs. In addition, a biting wind blew in curtains of water, and even the largest of umbrellas offered no protection.

His pant legs were soaked by the time they finally reached the grave site, striding through the somber and soggy grayness of the cemetery walkways. He began shaking twice at that place, but not from the freezing cold. First, he was horrified by the sight of four bareheaded figures in mouse-colored uniforms, soaking wet. Leaning

*on their shovels, with hauntingly blank stares, they were
waiting behind the pile of dug up earth which was quickly
turning to mud. What he then saw was even worse, when
he approached the actual grave just before the undertakers
were to lower the casket. The bottom was already full of
water.*

*As soon as they lifted the first shovelfuls of squishy dirt,
he turned and rushed toward the exit, barely restraining
himself from breaking into a run. He was completely re-
solved that he would never again step into a cemetery of
any kind.*

*That "never" had indeed lasted a long time, in human
terms: almost four decades.*

The funeral was at the same graveyard, but everything else was different. The autumn of that year had
been remarkably mild, and the cremation—without
grave or undertakers—took place on a bright sunny
day. No one looked at him crossly or reproached him,
as he had feared, for having missed so many funerals.
To the contrary, several people nodded and smiled discreetly at him during the service, and after it was over a
few of those who recognized him came up and greeted
him warmly, even though they had not seen him for
the longest time. They chatted, and someone even told
an anecdote about the deceased, which brought on a
brief muffled laugh.

He did not leave the cemetery with the others. He
headed away from the entrance, toward his father's
grave. He scarcely would have found it had he not
checked the plot number in the documents before
leaving. He didn't remember where it was located at
all. At the funeral he had just followed the carriage
with the coffin, paying no attention to the path they

took or where they turned. In his fuzzy memory, the gravestones he had passed by looked like shapeless dark boulders, surfacing here and there from the rain-soaked fog.

Now it was completely different. Yesterday's wind had blown away the dust, and the air had cleared. The autumn colors of the manicured bushes glittered in the sun. Upon the backdrop of this palette, dominated by green and yellow, it seemed that the marble was no longer an omen of death. The dates on the headstones spoke not of the fact that someone had died, but quite the opposite, that someone had lived.

Walking slowly, Mr. Rigoud felt an impression forming in his soul, one which he was convinced was most unsuitable for this place. He was surrounded by beauty. A special kind of beauty, for which one needs a special vision. With this insight there also came the sting of sadness. Did so many years have to pass for him to fathom the beauty of the graveyard?

His father's grave did not disturb the surrounding harmony. His son had not come to look after it, but the management had taken care of it. Not a single besmirching exception was allowed to desecrate the beauty of which this cemetery boasted. What an incredible turn of events, Mr. Rigoud thought excitedly, standing in the same spot he had taken as the undertakers had begun lowering the coffin into the water-filled grave. Then he had fled in horror; now it seemed to him that he might linger for a long time.

He had been standing thus for about fifteen minutes, when something occurred to him. He had to immortalize this special moment. The weather was already forecast to change the next day, autumn would again show its long-overdue dreary face, and it might be spring before the beauty of the cemetery once again shone forth. What's more, who knew when and whether he would come here again. He should remember his father's grave like this from now on. A photograph taken at this moment would be a perfect memento.

He took out his cell phone, spent some time looking for the best angle, and snapped the picture. He stared for a moment at the photo and finally nodded. That's fine. He had almost captured the beauty to its full. He put the telephone back in his pocket, laid his hand for a moment on the headstone, and turned to leave.

He had gone no more than a dozen steps when he suddenly stopped. The grave he was passing was so pretty he simply could not resist the temptation. Only after he had taken the photograph did he begin to wonder whether snapping pictures was even allowed at the cemetery. Probably no one could keep him from photographing his father's grave, but what about other people's? Even if taking photos was not explicitly forbidden, perhaps one should ask for permission.

He looked about. There was no one around. Only at the far end of the walkway, a couple was slowly moving away. Their backs turned, the old man and woman surely hadn't seen him. He looked carefully then at a nearby lamppost, but he did not see a camera there. And if they recorded him, so what? He could pretend that he was not taking pictures but using his cell phone for something else. The gadget did have many functions. In any case, they did not have the right to ask to see his pictures.

Before leaving the cemetery, he took nine more photos of exceptionally pretty graves. He waited for a moment when there were no people around, and held the phone surreptitiously. He had been quite impatient to look through the photos straight away, but caution won the day. Better not to tempt fate. Soon he would be in the metro where almost everyone would be fiddling with their cell phones and he certainly wouldn't stand out.

No one sat down next to him, so he allowed himself to look through them as soon as it turned out that he had never heard the voice of the woman who had seemed familiar to him.

He was satisfied with his results, considering the circumstances. Perhaps they would have turned out better if he'd had the opportunity to frame the shots more carefully, but primarily he'd had to make sure that no one noticed him taking photographs. In any case, even as it was, the beauty of the graves had largely been captured. They would all look even better on the large monitor at home. Smiling, he went on scrolling from one picture to the next.

He had already raised his thumb to move from the sixth to the seventh picture, when a particular detail caught his attention. He brought the phone closer to see it better, but that was not enough, so he magnified the picture by spreading two fingers. The enlarged central part of the photo filled the screen, and Mr. Rigoud stared at the golden inscription on the gray marble, webbed with white squiggly lines.

He was surprised at what he read there, but was even more astounded that he had not seen it when he took the picture. True, fixated on taking the pictures as quickly and discreetly as possible, he had not paid attention to the names of those buried, but still, he should have noticed that the deceased shared his name. And not just that. They had been born in the same year. His namesake had died this year, apparently not too long ago, judging from the fact that no sign of weathering could be seen on the headstone.

He reduced the picture and quickly went through the remaining photographs. Focused on the names on the headstones, he was hardly aware any more of the beauty of the graves. Then he went back to the sixth picture. He looked at it for a while, shaking his head. No, something was wrong here. No matter how distracted he had been, he could not have failed to notice his own name.

He exited the gallery, put the phone in the inside pocket of his jacket, got up and went to the carriage exit. He would return to the cemetery and find the grave of his namesake. He didn't really know why, or what else he might discover there that was not in the photo, but he had no better idea, and he simply could not forget the whole affair. He got out at the first station, crossed over to the other platform and waited for a train in the opposite direction.

He easily discovered the grave from the fifth photograph, along with the seventh, but the grave he had photographed sixth was nowhere to be found. He turned this way and that, looking intently all around; he even went down the neighboring walkways, although he was certain that he had never been there, all in vain. His namesake's grave seemed to have been swallowed up by the earth.

He stood for a while in the middle of one of the walkways, thinking about what to do, then headed for the guardhouse beside the entrance. Inside he found a small skinny man with thinning hair. Nearly the whole of one wall of the tiny office was taken up by a map of the graves, while framed photographs hung on the other walls.

Sitting at a desk by the window, the man looked up

from the book he was reading, then quickly stood up and came to meet the visitor.

"Ah, Mr. Rigoud, you're here!" he said with an uncommonly deep voice for someone of his size. "Welcome, welcome!"

He offered his hand. Mr. Rigoud shook it in confusion. The handshake went on for a while.

"Do you know me?" Mr. Rigoud inquired dubiously.

"Certainly. You were already here today. You visited your father's grave for the first time in a long time."

So that's what it's all about, thought Mr. Rigoud.

"You have no right to judge me. It's no one's business how often or how rarely I come to my father's grave. That's my own private affair."

"Yes, of course. I'm not judging you at all. Your visit to your father's grave is none of my business. I'm interested in what happened after that."

Mr. Rigoud looked at the guard for a few moments in silence.

"If you're talking about my taking photographs, I didn't know it was prohibited. You should put up a sign saying that it's forbidden, not stalk those taking pictures so that you can fine them afterwards. I refuse to pay, because no damage was done. The pictures never left my phone. I'll simply erase them, right here in front of you—and that will be that."

Mr. Rigoud reached for his telephone, but his movement was halted midway.

"You would erase beauty?" The man said this more quietly than before.

"What?" asked Mr. Rigoud, after another brief silence.

"Why did you take pictures of the headstones in the first place?"

"Because they are. . . They looked so. . . They are so. . ."

"Beautiful?"

A brief interval ensued before Mr. Rigoud answered affirmatively, also in a muffled voice, "Beautiful, yes."

The guard's face again lit up with a smile. "You can't imagine how rare it is for someone to see the beauty of this place. I have been here for almost half a century, and I've only met this many." He indicated the framed photographs on the three walls. "Thirty-seven."

Mr. Rigoud approached one of the walls and looked at several of the pictures. "Who are these people next to the headstones?"

"People like you, with a sense for a special kind of beauty. All of them deserved to be rewarded for their gift. Just as you will be as well."

"Rewarded?"

"Yes. Each one of them got their own day. The cemetery compensated all of them."

A short silence again followed.

"I don't understand. What kind of day?"

"A day when the cemetery belongs only to you. You'll see soon."

Mr. Rigoud suddenly felt dizzy. "That's all. . . very interesting. . . but I didn't come here because of a reward, but because. . ."

"Because you didn't manage to find the grave of your namesake. The grave you photographed sixth."

Mr. Rigoud squinted. "How did you know?"

"That doesn't matter now. Do you still wish to see it?"

"Yes, but it's nowhere to be found. I looked everywhere. . . ."

"It's here, don't worry. And not just one of them."

The guard turned toward the cemetery map on the wall opposite the window. "Can you guess how many graves there are here?"

Mr. Rigoud looked at the network of walkways and paths which criss-crossed the marked plots and shrugged. "I don't know. Certainly more than a hundred. . . Maybe two hundred. . ."

"Three hundred and fourteen. And all of them, every single one, will today have the same inscription. In your honor."

"The same inscription?"

"Yes, your name. Just like on the grave you saw."

Mr. Rigoud wanted to ask several questions at once, but one came to the fore.

"But I am alive. How can I have three hundred and fourteen graves?" He stopped suddenly. "Or perhaps I'm no longer alive?"

"You are alive, of course. More alive than you have ever been or ever will be again. Such a day of beauty will never repeat itself in your lifetime. And not an impersonal, nameless beauty at that, but one that bears your signifier. Your name. What could be more befitting?"

From the conscious thought of Mr. Rigoud, all the other questions which had been contending for precedence instantly disappeared. Not a single one of them was important anymore. Instead a new one formed, the only one that still made sense.

"What. . . what am I supposed to do?"

"You should spend your day at the cemetery. Go from grave to grave and photograph them. Slowly. Even though you'll enjoy it, it is a big job—to take three hundred and fourteen pictures of beauty. It will last until the late afternoon."

"But people will wonder. . . other visitors to the cemetery. . . The same name everywhere. . ."

"No one else will be here except you. The cemetery is already closed. As I said, today it belongs only to you."

Whilst he felt that there was no reason to hesitate, Mr. Rigoud stood looking at the guard unblinking, until the man gently placed his hand on Rigoud's shoulder.

"Go on ahead, Mr. Rigoud. I will be waiting for you here at the end. I also have a pleasant task to do in the meantime. I have to take and frame the thirty-eighth picture."

4. The Quadrangle

Miss Muriel Juillard, authoress—here she is in the picture—had in each season a special place where she would seek and occasionally find different sources of inspiration.

Every Saturday in winter, she would go in turn to one of the four large Parisian train stations: La Gare de l'Est, La Gare du Nord, Lyon or Montparnasse. She would sit in one of the cafés next to the window, from where there was a good view of the large open space. She would order a very sweet cappuccino and spend about an hour curiously watching the multitude of travelers whose life paths had briefly crossed, and even at times become interwoven here. This seemed to stimulate her into thinking about the circumstances in which chance tailors the fates of literary protagonists, which had always been the hardest part of her job as a writer.

During the spring, twice a month, she would visit one of the racetracks in the vicinity of Paris. She had no taste whatever for horseracing, nor anything else that she felt was cruel to animals. Nor was she attracted to gambling in the least, but she was truly interested in the gallery of human faces demonstrating the entire range of emotions, from excitement to hopelessness, from complete euphoria to ultimate boredom. In addition, she had an eye for the various details of clothing, shoes, hats and jewelry of the rather upper class people who gathered there. All this later proved useful when she was depicting the appearance of characters from high society who often appeared in her books.

In summer she spent two afternoons every month at the "Joséphine Baker" swimming pool. She would always go there on Mondays because it was least crowded. She would put on a one-piece bathing suit with a long, colorful, see-through tunic over it and light leather beach sandals, then lie down on a beach chair underneath an umbrella. She'd open a book, but not read it. She would watch people over the top of the thick volume, though this wasn't apparent because of her sunglasses. Of course, she was not interested in other people's nakedness, at least not their physical nakedness, but in the exposure of their souls which often accompanied it. Penetrating that bareness was the foundation of her prose style.

In the autumn she would head to the metro for her inspiration, also twice a month, but only then did she not have a predetermined day. She relied on the inner voice which would inform her when it was the right time to ride the same line from one end of the city to the other and back. During the ride, which lasted about fifty minutes in one direction, she would first select three passengers who somehow seemed to her the most literary, although, if someone were to ask her, she could not have explained what that meant exactly. There were always three because various kinds of triangles were the main form of her narrative geometry.

Usually these were not people who sat or stood near her. They were at the opposite end of the carriage, so that she might remain inconspicuous as she first watched and then photographed them. The camera in her cell phone had a powerful zoom, so it looked as if they had been photographed up close. She would frame the photographs and keep them on her desk the whole time she was writing the novel in which they played a central role.

The writing itself, although lasting for months, was the technical part of the job. That which preceded it, the composition of the story, lasted as long as the ride on the metro in both directions. After taking the pictures of the three passengers, she no longer paid any attention to them. They would go their own way, unaware that they had just entered the world of literature, while on her way back to her first stop, she would slowly scroll through the three pictures on her screen, observing carefully the strangers' faces.

Every such round-trip would help form a story in her mind, and only later, on her return home, would she decide whether one of them was good enough to be formulated into a novel. Very rarely did that happen, though. She would be pleased if, at the end of her autumnal sojourn in the metro, she had gained the inspiration for two books. A fertile year of writing then awaited her, until the following autumn.

On this day it seemed to her for a long while that her inner voice was mistaken. Almost half the outward ride had passed, and she still hadn't seen a single literary passenger. Well, perhaps the only exception was the elderly gentleman in the bright red sweater, immersed in his reading, all the way at the back of the carriage; but where was she to find two more people to go with him, when all the rest were so drab and average?

At that point, at the stop near the cemetery, another elderly gentleman dressed all in black entered the metro. What caught her attention, however, were not his mourning clothes, but rather something about his expression. The man was clearly coming back from a funeral, but his face looked radiant, as if he had just experienced something remarkably beautiful. Such paradoxes could be quite interesting in the world of literature.

If only a suitable lady would appear, the writer thought, the triangle would be complete. And indeed, at the very next stop, into the carriage came a lady of similar age, who, as it soon turned out, also possessed certain literary traits. Sitting down opposite the man buried in his reading, she not only tried to catch his attention in every possible way, but she didn't even hesitate openly to take his picture.

This reminded Miss Juillard that she should also take pictures. She took out her cell phone and discreetly snapped three shots. A moment later, she was already completely ignoring the three passengers at the other end of the carriage, focusing her attention on studying their photographs in search of the story which would best connect them.

As the stations passed by, all kinds of plots occurred to her. She had a lot of experience in creating love triangles; not surprisingly—she had written of nothing else for twenty-three years, ever since she had published her first book of prose.

Originally she had never intended to devote herself to this type of novel. It was incidental that her first book was about a vacation in Provence, during which the fate of two sisters was intertwined with the elder one's lover. She never told anyone that the story was inspired by personal experience.

The very first publisher she offered it to liked it, and

so did the readership. The publisher asked her to write a new novel, but did not accept the plot summary which she soon submitted because it was quite different from the plot of the first novel. Readers should be given tried and tested material, he explained to her, not something which might betray their expectations, no matter how good it was.

She did not agree right away, especially since the publisher initially suggested that she write a sequel to her first novel. How can there be a sequel, she asked him in disbelief, when two of the three protagonists have died at the end of the first book? No problem at all, the publisher replied, unfazed. Bring them back to life. She looked at him with such astonishment that he immediately changed his proposal. All right, there won't be a sequel, even though that would be best. But there has to be a new story about a love triangle. That's what readers expect of you.

She agonized for two days before she accepted the publisher's offer. It required a great deal for her to let go of her idealized vision of the writer's calling. If she wanted to be a published, popular, and in addition—which was not unimportant—a well-paid authoress, she must submit to the rules of the publishing industry game. For now she would write about love triangles, but it didn't have to be that way forever. Eventually she would get a chance to write about what she wanted.

She comforted herself with this thought whenever she signed a contract for a new book on the same old theme. Although she did not vary thematically, she was at least a prolific authoress. In slightly less than a quarter century, she had written as many as thirty-three novels about love triangles. With each of them she hoped it was the last one of its kind. When it turned out that it wasn't, she acquiesced to the constant loyalty of her readers and the comfortable life it made possible. However, her satisfaction was always tainted by a certain bitterness, which she found harder to swallow with each passing year.

The bitterness resurfaced suddenly now as she was looking at the three pictures and composing a plot for her new novel. It took her a while to realize what had caused her reaction: the age of the passengers in her pictures. She had never used elderly characters. All those stories about them forming in her mind dealt with ephemerality and pointlessness, unfulfilled hopes and missed opportunities. Her other novels too, those with younger characters, were indeed nostalgic and sentimental—which is probably why they especially appealed to women readers—but they were not as gloomy as this.

Miss Julliard was still two decades away from that period of life, but they would pass quickly, and she herself would confront unfulfilled hopes and missed opportunities. Unless she did something about it as soon as possible. Right away, in fact. She simply had to write a work with a different theme from the one given her, no matter what the consequences. After all, what was the worst that could happen? Her publisher could refuse to publish it. She'd find another. That wouldn't be difficult any more. And if she betrayed the expectations of her readership, hadn't she already written enough books which suited their taste? She certainly had the right to write one that would please her as well.

This decision dispelled the bitterness, but also confronted her with a new problem. What sort of novel was it that would please her? Was it perhaps that plot summary that her publisher had rejected so long ago?

No: today that immature story seemed entirely naive. What's more, it turned out that the publisher had actually done her a favor by not publishing it. She stopped scrolling through the three photos on the screen of her cell phone and started looking out the window at the wall of the metro tunnel which was rushing by. No matter how hard she tried, no idea occurred to her.

She continued looking outside even once they had entered a tiny station with almost no passengers. As the ride went on, a strange impression overcame her. She had seen something at the station which seemed to be connected with the subject she had been contemplating so deeply. She realized what it was only after they had reached the next stop, and she saw again the wall ad touting a large white rectangle with bright red edges.

Of course! She must change the basic geometric figure of her books, abandon the triangle which so terribly inhibited her. Later, if she decided to write what she wanted, she could add as many sides as she liked, but for a start, just one would be enough. For now she needed nothing more than a rectangle. One more central character along with the three she already had.

She looked down the carriage to see if there was a fourth passenger with literary traits. At first she noticed that, of the first three, the only one left was the gentleman who still never looked up from his book. She had not seen when the aggressive woman and the man in mourning had left, but that wasn't important. She had already taken their pictures. Unfortunately, although she thoroughly examined about fifteen faces, not a single one seemed in the least literary. Well, there was nothing to be done; she must be patient. Three or four stops remained till the end of the line, and then the whole trip would head in the opposite direction. With luck someone interesting would turn up.

Again she looked into the darkness between the stops. Actually, it was only semi-dark. The window pane acted as a mirror. It was enough just to change the focal distance a little and the wall of the tunnel turned into a black backdrop against which one saw the inside of the carriage. The scene was dominated by her own face, but for a long while it was as if she was unaware of it. It was only after two stops that it finally dawned on her that she was looking not at her own face, but at a truly literary one. It was exactly the one she needed.

She came to when the magic dispersed upon entering the next-to-last stop. Whilst there was actually no reason to hurry, her movements were feverish as she moved her hand away from herself, preparing to do something she had never done before and which she found deeply repulsive: to take a selfie.

She did so quickly and, she hoped, unnoticed. She smiled for a second, snapped the picture, and held the phone to her breast. When the train set off for the last stop, she held it just far enough away that she alone could see the photograph, as if there were others around her interested in what was on her phone.

This time her smile lingered. The picture confirmed what the window pane had suggested. Story after story could be told just about this face, and when related to the others, that would be the novel she had never written. As they neared the end of the line, she looked at the four photographs, relishing the chance to start constructing her first rectangular plot summary as soon as the train left again in the opposite direction.

The final stop became the first when most of the previous passengers were replaced by new ones. The train stood for a few minutes. The sliding doors finally began to close, but before they met in the middle, someone suddenly knocked on the window next to which Miss Julliard was sitting. She turned in bewilderment. However, she did not manage to see anything because of the flash of a camera from the other side of the glass.

She was left blinded and angered. She had read about various unpleasant incidents in the metro, of which there seemed to be more and more recently. Although she rode the metro often, nothing bad had ever happened to her. If it was now her turn, she had gotten off easy. This was most likely some joker and not an attacker. Some obviously immature guy wanted to frighten innocent passengers by setting a flash off in their faces. With luck the station cameras had caught him.

She was still seeing stars a little when they reached the second station. She needed to focus on her work as soon as possible. She didn't dare allow a minor incident to disrupt such an important moment. She was looking at the passengers who were still getting on, when all of a sudden she became aware that someone was standing next to her window and watching her. She turned her head quickly and saw a young man who was just then raising his cell phone. She squinted in anticipation of another flash, but this time there was none. Having taken her picture, the young man lowered his phone. He did not walk away. Smiling, he went on looking at her. She looked back at him, but only briefly, because the train set off the next instant.

On any other occasion, she would first have been overcome with resentment, wondering why a gang of weirdos had chosen her of all people as their victim. They had spread out along the metro line she was on and for some reason they had decided to photograph her, perhaps even at every station. Then she would have become afraid, thinking that they were not oddballs at all but that this all had something to do with her writing. She would have remembered how a group of readers had manhandled recently a certain writer just because they didn't like the fate he intended for his protagonist at the end of a certain book. The poor fellow had wound up in the hospital. These were dangerous times for writers.

Now, however, as the train rushed toward the third station, she felt neither resentment nor fear. The smiling young man had been neither a weirdo nor an angry reader. He was no danger. She was sure of it because he wasn't a stranger to her. She could have sworn to it, even though she couldn't remember where she knew him from. However, she had no time to dig deeper into her memory because they soon came upon the third station, and there she was met by a new surprise.

As the train pulled in, she turned to face the window. When the train stopped, three young people were standing before Miss Julliard: the young man from the previous station and two girls dressed in the fashion of, say, a quarter century ago. The smaller of the two girls took a camera from her little purse, smiled at the traveler in the metro and took her picture. Nothing else happened until the train pulled out. Then all three waved at her. She waved back at them with a slight hesitancy, so she wasn't sure if they had seen her, but that wasn't really important. Their parting—she somehow knew—wouldn't last long. They would already be waiting for her again at the next station.

The women's summer wear did what the three faces couldn't—it revived her memory. She did not immediately recognize the boy first and then the girls, because she had never actually seen them. They were only figments of her writer's imagination. She had conjured them up by making them as different as possible from reality, so that she could hide the fact that her first novel was autobiographical. To accomplish this, it had not been necessary to change the clothes as well, so the girl who had just taken her picture had been dressed just like the young Miss Julliard that summer long ago in Provence.

What will happen at the next station, she wondered as the train rushed through a fresh tunnel. Would the second girl also take her picture now? Perhaps, but that wouldn't be all. This performance—she guessed—must have some deeper meaning, not just the taking of pictures. She expected them to appear again at her window, she turned in readiness in that direction, but she didn't see them there. They were a little further back, near the door. Bright faces, they beckoned to her to get off the train.

If there had been time to hesitate, she would certainly have thought twice about it. However, trains stopped only briefly at small stations like this one, so she had no time for dilemmas. She practically jumped out of her seat and rushed toward the door, which closed as soon as she had stepped out onto the platform.

As the train accelerated, departing the empty station, the three young people gathered around her. No one said anything, they just smiled. When the train disappeared into the tunnel, the girl who was dressed as the younger Miss Julliard first gracefully raised her hand and stroked her hair and then her face. Next the other two followed her example.

The writer didn't usually like to be touched, especially by strangers. But these were no strangers. Who was closer or more dear to her than the three of them? Nonetheless, it took a while before she gathered the courage to reciprocate. As she ran her fingers over the smooth skin of their faces and their sumptuous hair, she was overcome by a feeling that she had not had for a long, long time: elation.

Then she began to hear a clamor from somewhere. She quickly withdrew her hand, as if she might be caught doing something improper, and looked around the station. There was still no one except the four of them, but now she realized where the sounds were coming from. A larger group of people was coming down the three concourses which, on their side of the tracks, led to and from the platform. For an instant she looked at the girls and the young man in anxious doubt, but they just kept smiling.

As if they had agreed when to appear, people began pouring out of the three concourses in the same instant. A great mixture of men and women rushed toward the middle of the platform where the small group was standing. While they took their places around them, camera flashes were going off all around. Aimed at Miss Julliard, they drove her to squint. Finally, when it seemed everyone had arrived, filling up the central section of one side of the station, applause broke out.

This time, the writer had no difficulty remembering. She recognized unmistakably each of the ninety-six faces, although she had never seen them in real life either—the three main protagonists from each of her other thirty-two triangular novels. Such a nice round number, she thought. With the four of them here, it was exactly one hundred, which meant as many as twenty-five quadrangular novels with the new division of roles. She would have her hands full until she reached the age of unfulfilled hopes and missed opportunities.

She herself started clapping.

5. Selfie

MR. ALEXANDRE LECLAIR—WHOM YOU see in the picture—would certainly have paid no attention to the unassuming woman sitting diagonally across from him, next to the window on the other side of the metro carriage, had it not been for the strange way she took a selfie. The lady could have been twice the age of Mr. Leclair, who had just turned twenty. She had short straight hair, and she was dressed in a simple gray suit with a light-colored blouse to match.

She accomplished it quite quickly. She suddenly stretched out her left hand, holding her rather large cell phone in front of her, flashed a smile accompanied by a shutter sound, and then at equal speed hugged the phone to her chest. She held it there for a while, finally raising it, but just enough that she alone could see the picture even though no one was sitting next to her.

What's all the hurry and the obvious embarrassment about, Mr. Leclair asked himself. You'd think the lady was shy. Not a few people considered it narcissistic and generally improper to take pictures of themselves, especially if they were no longer young. Why, he was still young, and he was no fan of selfies either. But if that were the case, why did she decide to take one in the metro anyway, where so many people would be watching? True, it seemed that her sneak selfie shot had gone unnoticed by anyone but him, but someone else might have seen. Why risk it?

Or perhaps she was facing a problem similar to his own? A chill ran down his spine at the thought. He immediately wanted to sit down next to the unknown woman and start up a conversation with her. Although, even if he was right in supposing that they might both benefit, he still could not frighten her like that. If it turned out that there was some simpler explanation for her demeanor, he would look not just like a pest, but a madman.

For now it would be best just to keep a discreet eye on her. The last station was coming up, but she remained in her seat as if she intended to go on riding. He didn't mind at all, he would stay too, for as long as necessary. If they had the same trouble, it might exhibit itself in some other way, and then he would approach her without hesitation. He so longed to come across a kindred spirit. He had almost convinced himself that his case was unique, that the trouble truly was in his head.

It had all started apparently innocently the Saturday before. He'd had no intention whatsoever of going to the flea market, but Valerie had insisted. The day was fine, one should be outside as much as possible, and the turnout was best over the weekend at Les Puces de Montreuil. He thought she needed something in particular, but after an hour and a half of walking around the market, she was still just browsing.

"Don't worry, I'll find something," she responded to his comment that she would end up buying nothing. "I never come home from the flea market empty-handed."

The main trouble with Valerie was that she never shut her mouth. If it hadn't been for her excessive babbling, they would probably have been in a permanent relationship by now and not a more-or-less casual one. They liked each other in the spirit of the principle that opposites attract. He was skinny and gangly, fair-haired, and she was tiny and round, almost like a ball; her chestnut hair grew down to her waist.

The young man's reticence was just one more item in the list of harmonious opposites between them, but after some time, the girl's ceaseless talking had begun to get on his nerves. She didn't stop even while they were making love. Still, since the sex was otherwise more than satisfactory, they were still together.

Alexandre bought a camera just to shut Valerie up for a while. They went from stall to stall, and whilst she had something to say to almost every seller, she was not in the least interested in what most of them had to offer. She certainly didn't need a camera because she already had one which she didn't even use, preferring the one in her cell phone. Still, she stopped in front of a stall covered with used cameras and started asking the bald middle-aged owner about the features and prices of the merchandise on offer.

At first the man answered patiently, but after the seventh or eighth camera, when he finally realized that the girl was just leading him on, he frowned and started responding with increasing frustration, especially since a young man had approached the stall who seemed to be a more serious customer. Valerie, apparently, was oblivious to all this, but tirelessly went on asking questions. Alexandre had to do something in order to prevent the row that was about to break out. He reached into his pocket, pulled out a bill, offered it to the seller and wordlessly pointed to the camera he remembered to be the cheapest.

"Why did you buy that?" Valerie asked in confusion once they had stepped away from the stall.

"I need it," came the concise answer.

"For what?"

"To take pictures."

"But you have your phone. No one takes pictures with a camera anymore."

"The camera in my phone is no good," Alexandre answered in unusually wordy fashion.

"It can't be any worse than this thing. Anyway, you would have done better to upgrade and buy a new cell phone."

The discussion ended here because they had arrived at the next stall. Valerie immediately got into a conversation with the vendor of old records, though they interested her even less than used digital cameras. For a start, she didn't even own a record player. Finally she managed to buy an old 45 for almost nothing, because she liked the fading cover.

"There, you see," she said proudly. "Didn't I tell you I would find something?"

Returning home, Mr. Leclair put the camera on the cabinet and forgot about it. He didn't remember it till the early evening, when his eye fell upon that piece of furniture. Since he wasn't busy doing anything, he picked it up and looked at it a bit. He didn't manage to turn it on, however. So, it seemed he had been sold a pup. It served him right for buying at the flea market, and not checking it out before paying. Fortunately he hadn't paid much; he would survive the loss. Whatever the case, Valerie must not find out about it.

He would tell her that he'd tried it and that it really was poorer than the camera in his cell phone. That would please her. Valerie loved to be right. It would be best to throw it straight in the trash so that she wouldn't get the idea of going back to the flea market and entering into an argument with the bald guy, trying to return the camera to him. And what else could he do with the it? If he took it to be repaired, he would just go on wasting money. Valerie was actually right— in that case it would be better to get a new cell phone.

He was already heading for the kitchen when he became aware that the camera was lighter than one would expect. He hadn't noticed when he'd first picked it up at the flea market, nor when he'd taken it off the chest of drawers a few minutes before. He opened the lid on the battery compartment and sighed. Well, of course! Who in the world includes batteries with a device at the flea market?

He didn't have any spare batteries, and he didn't want to go to the store to buy new ones, so he took two from the TV remote. They were, to be fair, on their last legs, but they would be good enough to take a picture or two with the flash. He smiled when the old camera came to life.

He thought a bit about what to photograph, then pointed the lens at the chest of drawers. There were several little things of various colors on it. Just perfect for a trial run. He snapped one picture, then another half a minute later. He turned the camera over and studied the options. The first of the two pictures soon appeared on the little screen. Valerie wouldn't like this. The photo was significantly better than one he might take with his cell phone.

If he had turned off the camera then, he would have saved himself a lot of headaches later. He had no reason to look at the second picture. The first by itself was enough for the trial run; he could have been satisfied just to know that the camera worked well, and then put it in one of the messy drawers of the cabinet and forgotten about it, as happened with so much other junk that ended up in there.

The two photos should have been identical. He had taken them from the same spot within a short time. However, that was not the case. When he looked at the second picture, everything was the same as in the first, except that one of the little figures on the cabinet had disappeared. He stared at the screen, but he couldn't remember what had been there before, so he went back to the first picture. In the middle of the cabinet, out of nowhere, appeared the wooden figure of a three-headed elephant which one of his friends had brought him from a trip to Cambodia.

He looked up from the camera to the chest of drawers. The dusty little figure was standing there where he had put it when he first got it. He took it in his free hand, turned it about and looked at it, then put it back. He focused again on the camera. Like a child who has gotten a new toy, he began to flip between the two photos, watching how the three-headed elephant appeared and disappeared.

Suddenly the screen went black. He tried to turn the camera on, but couldn't. He sighed for a second time. He would have to go to the store.

He returned from there with a pack of six batteries. On any other occasion he would first have reinstated the remote and put away the two extras, but now that had to wait. He quickly put the new batteries into the camera and aimed it at the cabinet, only to change his mind. He looked around the living room, went over to the bookshelf and took a shot of it up close. He'd intended to take one more, but then he changed his mind again. He would look at the first straight away.

He expected, like an analogy of the pictures of the cabinet, that everything would be in order, but it was not. In the series of books there was a gaping hole which was filled in front of him by a thick volume. He pulled it out a little, just to touch it, and then pushed it back in. He stood unmoving for a while, then finally raised the camera and started taking pictures from the top to the bottom.

Even though the bookshelf was completely full, a book was missing from each of the nine rows. He patiently checked which books had vanished. Inspired by his recollection of a novel he had once read, he thought that some meaning might be hiding there. If there was any, he couldn't figure it out. Then something else occurred to him, so he took pictures of the rows again. His premonition turned out to be true this time. Again, in each photograph one book was missing, but not the same one as in the previous picture of that row.

When Valerie arrived around nine-thirty, she found him sitting and ruminating on the couch in the living room, holding the camera he had bought at the flea market. During the preceding two and a half hours, he had taken one hundred and ninety-six pictures throughout the apartment. It turned out to be a good thing he had bought six batteries, because the flash drained them quickly. In the camera was the last, the third pair, and even they were already almost expended. He would soon have to put them in the remote if Valerie wanted to watch television.

Something was missing in every picture. It was rarely one of the larger objects. (The largest was a framed poster in the hallway.) Mainly small things disappeared, their absence not always easy to notice. Once his original excitement had settled and no explanation for the strange phenomenon had appeared, it had all turned into a kind of game.

As a boy, he had loved to solve a popular puzzle in a kids' magazine: two seemingly identical pictures were different in ten details that needed to be discovered. Here, the difference between reality and the photograph was just one detail, but sometimes he had to invest a lot of effort in order to find it. He quickly began to experience the used camera as an opponent against which he was doing battle.

Valerie acted like she always did when she had been gone for the least little while: the moment she stepped through the door she started talking in great detail about what had happened to her while they had been apart. Despite the fact that, almost without exception, her experiences were uninteresting, Alexandre would listen patiently to her, because not only was he a caring person, he was also convinced it would be hard, even impossible, to interrupt her. Now, however, he must attempt the impossible.

He offered her the camera and nodded at the library. "Take pictures of the books."

Still talking, Valerie took the camera and pointed it at the shelf.

"A little closer."

She moved closer and snapped the picture.

"One more time."

She gave him a glum stare before taking the second picture. Then she handed the camera back and headed for the kitchen, from where she went on talking a little louder so that he wouldn't miss anything.

No longer listening to her, Alexandre quickly looked at the two new photos. There were no empty spaces among the books. In both pictures, all the books were in place. He stared at the screen for a few more seconds before pushing the button to turn it off. He took out the batteries and put them in the remote, then got up and put the camera away in the bottom drawer of the cabinet.

Just as he sat down again, Valerie came out of the kitchen carrying a bottle of wine and two glasses. Only then did he become aware that she had finished talking.

"What's on TV?" she asked, setting the bottle and glasses on the coffee table in front of the couch.

Valerie was still asleep when he left the apartment the next morning. First he bought two packs of six batteries each, although he certainly didn't need that many. He would not have to use the flash during the day, nor did he plan to take a multitude of pictures like he had the previous evening. Just a few would be enough to check what happened when he took pictures outside.

He worked that out with the very first picture, but he did not stop taking them until he completely filled up the memory, some time after one in the afternoon. Again it was a battle of wits with the camera. The photographs being now more expansive, little things did not disappear, but often it was not easy to figure out what large object was missing. He needed a good eye to notice what had vanished: which tree from the line of trees, which road sign or traffic light, which parked car, which chair from the courtyard of a café, which company name from above a shop window. Architectural ornaments went missing from the façades of buildings, smaller windows, narrow passages, and even the whole roof from a three-story building which became flat on top in the picture. He had the most trouble with a tiny cloud which stood as if anchored in a patch of sky above the street, but it was not there in the picture.

He had interrupted his photo session for about twenty minutes when Valerie called him around eleven-thirty to ask where he had gone so early on a Sunday. He answered honestly, although incompletely. He had gone out to take a few pictures with the camera he had bought the day before at the flea market. That seemed to satisfy her, so she immediately changed topic to one more interesting for her: the morning news from her life. He listened to her, standing on a corner somewhere and occasionally nodding his head. Once the report was finished, he realized that this break, in fact, had been a welcome one. Taking the photos, and especially figuring them out, was fairly exhausting.

Returning home at about one-thirty, he wondered if he should tell Valerie about all this. He concluded that it still wasn't time to do so. He couldn't offer her any sort of explanation, so it would just upset and probably frighten her. It could turn out even more unpleasantly, since the camera behaved normally in her hands, while in his it became abnormal.

Still, he showed her the pictures from the streets. She, of course, saw nothing unusual in them. She looked at several of them, announced that they weren't bad, but that it still would have been better for him to buy a new cell phone. He agreed with her.

Even though he had classes on Monday, he stayed home. He waited for Valerie to go to the university, then set up the computer and started searching. He stopped only when she returned in the late afternoon. His hours of searching were fruitless. Nowhere on the internet could he find even a mention of anything similar to the enigma he was facing. It was as if no one else in the world had ever had to do with such a strange camera. Or at least, no one had left a mention of it. It didn't even show up as a theme in literary works.

He spent a restless night, often waking from nightmarish dreams that he could not remember. Unlike him, Valerie always remembered with ease what she had dreamt and never missed a chance to recount her dreams to him first thing in the morning. Listening with one ear over breakfast, he wracked his brain about what he could possibly do next. He hardly ate a bite. Drinking his second cup of coffee, he suddenly stopped in mid-air as he brought the cup to his lips, as a simple solution occurred to him.

The best thing would be to do nothing at all. He would simply erase all the pictures and thus remove every trace of the puzzle. It would be perfect if he could also get rid of the camera itself, but how could he explain its disappearance to Valerie if she started asking about it for some reason? She might, let's say, get the idea she wanted to use it on some occasion, even though she didn't rate it much. Such contradictions were common to her.

He waited for Valerie to go to the bathroom and then erased all the photos and put the camera in the chest of drawers. It could just stay there. It was important that it was no longer in front of him, like a reminder of the trouble he had gotten into. He would manage to get rid of it after some time had passed and Valerie had forgotten about it.

Even though the camera was no longer visible, his restless interrupted dreams did not cease. He put up with them for three more nights, but by Friday morning it was clear to him that nothing would come of burying his head in the sand. He could not solve the problem by just pretending that it didn't exist. Even though out of sight, the camera hovered constantly before his eyes. It turned out for the best, actually, that he had not thrown it away. If he had, he would have been left without the last trail that might lead him to a solution.

He waited again for Valerie to go to the university, and then he dug the camera out of the chest of drawers. He inserted new batteries, just in case, although he did not intend to take pictures. He put on his windcheater and headed for the metro station.

He had no idea how to get information about the previous owner from the bald stallholder, but with luck he would figure something out on his way to the flea market. Whatever the case, he wouldn't mention what had happened to him. The man would certainly conclude that he was crazy, and refuse to help him. The worst scenario would be if he knew nothing, but he had to hope this wasn't the case, because otherwise he had no way of finding out if someone else had also experienced this, or if all this trouble was, in fact, in his head.

He envied Valerie. If something like this had happened to her, she would simply have gotten rid of the camera—thrown it away, left it somewhere, given it to someone—and gone on calmly living her everyday life. Not all inexplicable phenomena had to be explained for a person to be happy. She certainly would not have been haunted by nightmares.

The lady in the gray suit, whom he was clandestinely watching, scrolled a little through the pictures on her cell phone as they drew close to the last station. She then looked around the carriage as if searching for someone. Her eyes brushed across Mr. Leclair. Of course!—he realized at that moment. The lightning fast selfie was actually a sign. She was currently checking whether some kindred spirit had noticed it. Instead of waiting for her to indicate somehow that she was suffering from difficulties similar to his, he should have answered her without hesitating. To send her a sign of his own.

He took the camera from the pocket of his windcheater and turned it on at the very moment that the woman looked his way again. Not bothering to smile, he took a selfie even more quickly than she had about ten minutes before. (His too, he hoped, counted as a selfie, even though it wasn't taken with a cell phone.)

Following her lead, he held the screen to his chest for a little while. When he finally raised it, he did it the same way she had, just a little, even though there was no one sitting next to him either. But even if there had been, it would have made no difference—as he saw immediately—because there was nothing to hide. There was no selfie. Everything else could be seen: an empty seat, the back of the head of the man sitting behind him, the other passengers who had entered at the station of departure in the meantime. Only he was missing.

6. Memories

Mrs. Maryse Bouvet—here she is in the picture—was mildly surprised at first. The skinny young man in the windcheater, who had been sitting across from her in the metro, seemed to have vanished mysteriously. She didn't see what had happened to him because she briefly turned her head toward the window. When she looked back into the carriage again, the seat across from her was empty, and the sliding door had just shut.

It hadn't seemed like he intended to get off. He had been leisurely making use of his camera. He must have changed his mind at the last moment and rushed out. How had he managed to do it so quickly, so unnoticed and so silently, like a magician? She got up, hoping to see him somewhere at the station, but the train set off, robbing her of the opportunity.

She sat back down and continued to look out the window, even once they had entered a tunnel. They were well on their way when she was once again surprised, this time more than mildly. Lost in thought about the young man's unusual disappearance, she stared for a full minute at the blurry reflection of her face in the glass, against the dark background of the tunnel wall, before she became aware that she did not recognize the woman she was looking at. That was not her reflection at all.

What kind of optical illusion could this be? The face of some other female passenger lay before her, also staring out of the train. She must be sitting somewhere further down in the carriage, because there was no such person anywhere near her. Maybe even in the next carriage. Still, she had never heard of a mirage in the metro.

Thinking that an announcement should be made about this so that passengers did not get confused, Mrs. Bouvet shook her head. The reflection in the window made the same motion. She sat still for a few seconds, then slowly nodded her head. Once more the reflection simultaneously did the same. Before she could try again—just in case, although it was already clear to her that there was no need—they entered a station and its lighting dispersed the improvised mirror.

How is this possible, she wondered. First she was overcome by confusion on receiving proof that she had been looking at herself after all, then by frustration because she could no longer do so. That surely could not have been her. The reflection was a bit blurry, true enough, but there was no doubt that Mrs. Bouvet did not look like that at all. Her face, her hair were both quite different.

She blinked hard. They were different, to be sure, but in what way exactly? She strained to imagine her own face, but in vain. That didn't worry her much. Most people find it difficult to conjure up their own countenance, let alone describe themselves. She did have to know, however, what her hair was like. Is there any woman who does not know that? And the only thing about which she had more of a hunch than actually knew, was that her hair was not like the reflection in the window.

Impatiently she waited for the train to move on

once again between stations, hoping that the face in the glass would change, that she would recognize herself, regardless of the fact that she wasn't sure what she looked like. However, nothing changed in the new tunnel. She was met by the same unknown reflection. Not knowing what to do, she continued to gaze at it, enchanted, until they reached the next station. There she finally snapped out of her trance, realizing that she couldn't just go on riding like this, staring at the window-mirror. If nothing else, she would eventually have to leave the metro.

This simple certainty confronted her, however, with a new problem, bigger than those preceding. She suddenly realized that she had no idea at which station she was supposed leave. Where was she going anyway? She frowned in accord with her reflection, straining to remember, but without success.

Very strange, she said to herself, finally looking away from the window. Such things happen only to those who are truly demented. They forget where they are going. Yet she was not suffering from dementia. At least as far as she knew. Then a new thought scared her a little. If she did, in fact, have difficulty remembering, then she probably wouldn't even realize. Those who are overcome by Alzheimer's have no recollection that they suffer from that disease.

Some time passed as she thought through all these terrible possibilities. Fortunately, she now had plenty of time. If you can't remember where you're going, then you're not in a hurry to get anywhere. You can reflect on things in peace. She focused on the unexpected problem, and two stations later she concluded that her choices had been narrowed. If she didn't know how to go forward, then all she could do was to go back.

Here, however, a new surprise lay in wait for her. It turned out that she knew just as much about going back as about going forward. Nothing.

She couldn't remember how she had ended up in the metro, at which station she had entered, where she had come from, where she lived. Did she live alone or with someone, did she have a family, was she married? Did she have kids? How old was she? Even though she was sitting down, it felt as if someone had pulled the carpet from under her. There was no past behind her, as if she had never lived up until now.

She was horrified, but also angered. If advanced Alzheimer's was in question, then there was no way she could be living alone. Someone would have to be looking after her. Whoever that was—her husband, one of the children, a relative, a care-giverr—certainly didn't dare allow her to take off on a metro ride all by herself. Or let her to sneak out, if that was what had happened.

How was she now to find her way home, when she knew absolutely nothing about herself? Should she ask the police for help? They would also be helpless because they wouldn't be able to identify her. If she only had some kind of ID with her. She was already in quite a panic when it occurred to her that she wasn't perhaps without documents. She had a black leather purse in her lap. Considering Mrs. Bouvet's state of mind, it was no wonder that she hadn't remembered to look inside it right away.

As she opened it feverishly, it crossed her mind that she might not have to talk to the police after all. If her ID card was in her purse, she would find her address and go there by herself. She would hold the document the whole time as a reminder of where she was going, so she wouldn't forget along the way.

However, there was nothing in her purse except a small red camera.

She observed it for a few moments, then carefully took it out, as if it might harm her somehow. She tested it briefly. It was simple to operate, though it shouldn't have seemed so to her. Alzheimer's patients forget what things are for and how they are used. She didn't spend time figuring out how she knew, in any case. Best to accept this positive circumstance without too much curiosity.

She turned the camera on. She expected to see the part of the carriage in front of her on the screen, in the direction that the lens was pointed. Instead, a picture taken earlier appeared. She hunched over to see it better.

As soon as her vision of the photograph sharpened, her memory returned. She should have been fairly surprised by that. How did that happen? And then also, how had the camera gotten into her bag? Finally, where did this picture in it come from? Still, her excitement at recognizing the photo dampened her wonderment.

Two grown-ups and three children smiling in a pose on the beach at Saint Raphaël. First on the left, Thierry, the father, then without a mustache or beard, still slim; next to him, wearing large earphones, Anthony their older son, who was about to start the lycée in the fall; then Théo, four years younger, his mouth smudged with the ice cream he was eating; nine year-old Laura, with a wide-brimmed straw hat and a big lollipop; last on the right, Maryse, the mother, with a colorful beach bag over her shoulder, enjoying a moment of carefree relaxation.

It was their last summer vacation together. The next year, Anthony would go to the seaside with his new friends from school.

Did the camera have other pictures from Saint Raphaël, Mrs. Bouvet wondered. They'd taken a lot of pictures that summer. She pushed the button with the right arrow.

A new rush of memories again buffered her wonderment. If it hadn't, she would have had even more reason to be surprised than the first time. Where had this other family come from? Had she perhaps gotten married twice? She obviously hadn't, because in this picture she was the same age as in the first, and bigamy was, of course, excluded as a possibility.

Standing next to the railing of a hotel terrace in Chamonix, with Mont Blanc looming in the background. The snow is shining bright. Although he does not ski, Patrick has dressed appropriately to be in accord with his three ladies in the photograph. Already a large man, in his ski suit he looks like a bear. In the middle are the twins, Catherine and Clair. The month before they had turned fourteen. When, like now, they are dressed the same, and with their skiing goggles hiding half their faces, not even their parents can tell between them. Catherine was supposed to wear her ski-pass on her left arm and Claire on the right, but who could be sure that they'd kept the deal? They enjoy it when people cannot tell them apart. For the picture, Maryse has pushed her sunglasses up on top of her head, and she is squinting in the afternoon sun.

Later that day, Catherine had fallen and injured her ankle. It was not broken, but they still had to put a low plaster boot on her leg. Claire had insisted that she also got one. In the end, she got her way by threatening to injure herself on purpose like her sister.

As she moved her thumb to press the button again

and change the picture, Mrs. Bouvet guessed what she would see, so she wasn't surprised when a third family photo appeared on the screen. The new memory suppressed an even greater wonderment: how could all these different pasts seem to be equally real, when all of them could not be?

They are at the zoo in Vincennes, next to the fenced in area with camels. Claude and Maryse are holding Simon, who was about to turn eight. Fatigue can be seen in the father's face. He has been patiently answering all the son's persistent questions for more than two hours. The mother is frowning, the stench of the large animals bothers her, and she is nervous because the weather is changing.

Salvation for the grown-ups was to come shortly, in the form of a sudden downpour. When they reached the car they were sopping wet, but also relieved. Yet they would pretend to be sad, like their son, because a higher power had interrupted their tour of the zoo.

When she recognized the scene in the next picture, she again failed to be surprised. She only thought about how unusual this was: just a little while before, she couldn't remember anything, as if she were being controlled by Alzheimer's, and now she had many more memories than normal. Here was a fourth life that she remembered quite well. Still, she wasn't sure if she should be proud of the memory.

Maryse and Jean-Marc are sitting at an ordinary wooden table with a checkered tablecloth in front of the "Chez René" tavern, in the little town of Baignant next to Pommard. The chairs are rickety, the evening is humid, the song of crickets comes from all around. They would have no reason to show up in this backwater if it weren't for the excellent wine. Jean-Marc is raising his glass, smiling broadly, seemingly a man without a care in the world. Maryse is trying to create the same impression, but a hardly noticeable shadow is darkening her face. He still didn't know that he only had three months to live at most. She would keep that from him as long as she could. That was the best way. He should enjoy life while he could.

That evening, in the little room above the tavern, they made love in a special way. Or at least it seemed so to her. Afterwards, as Jean-Marc quietly snored beside her, she cried for a long time. Quietly. If only they had had children, but he was unable to be a father, and she'd objected to the other ways of making a family. She would be alone next winter. She trembled at the idea, in spite of her sweating, despite the heat and humidity.

Before she looked for a new photograph, she became aware of a pattern that had escaped her till then. In each picture there was one person less. In the first there had been five, in the second four, then three, then two. That would mean. . .

She was sitting on a bench not far from Paris's Palais de Justice. In her left hand she was holding a tuna sandwich half wrapped in cellophane. With her right she was holding open a thick file in her lap. Next to her stood a plastic coffee cup with a lid. The next trial was to begin in twenty-five minutes. She had just enough time to grab a bite—she hadn't managed to eat breakfast that morning—and to leaf through the case documents one more time. This was to be her fourth case that day, and she had the same number in the afternoon. Then she would head to the office to prepare for the next day. She would only arrive home around nine. A shower, a quick meal, a glass of wine, maybe a little television or reading, if she wasn't overcome with fatigue, then off to sleep. The next day was to be equally stressful. Success as a lawyer demands that a person give their all. She had no time for a private life.

As she rushed off to court soon after, she would make an important decision. She would get an aquarium and some fish. They demanded the least attention. It was enough just to feed them twice a day. That way the apartment wouldn't be empty when she got home at night.

What will happen after this one, Mrs. Bouvet wondered. There cannot be less than one. There could not be a picture from which she was also absent. What sense would that make? Out of curiosity she pushed the button, but nothing happened. There was no photograph to bring back her sixth memory.

At first she was relieved. Six memories really would be too many. But then she suddenly realized there was no reason to be relieved. It actually made no difference if there were five or six. She could live with only one memory. Two were already excessive, so how was she to cope ultimately with the extra four? When she thought about it more carefully, this was much worse than Alzheimer's. Oblivion was undoubtedly far easier to put up with than an overabundance of memories. One could live with that, more or less.

If she could just choose one of the pasts. Even if she could, which one should she choose? And if she did choose one, what would happen to all the others? The moment she asked that question, it seemed like a horrible weight bore down on her. By choosing one past, the others would inevitably be destroyed. She would annihilate the lives in them. Not just her four lives—she could somehow stand that, because she simply couldn't live simultaneously in five versions—but the multitude of lives of her most loved ones. The lives of her children, her husbands. For her, they were all undeniably real. She remembered all of them perfectly.

Her hands began shaking as she held the camera. She looked at them as if they were someone else's, unable to stop them from trembling. Even if she'd actually had the chance to choose one of the five pasts, she absolutely could not have done so. No sane human being would be capable of making that horrible choice. Perhaps some ultimately merciless, unfeeling god could. Or indifferent chance. On the other hand, she could not hold onto all these pasts; she could go on living only in one. Where then was the exit from this dead end? Did one even exist?

The train was just entering a new station, when she was suddenly overcome by the impression that her remembrance of five pasts was not as complete as she thought. Something had escaped her. She realized what it was the moment the train set off again. Everything had been included, every detail from five lives, except for a surname. Now that's strange, she thought. How can something so important not be known? She clenched her eyes tight, and strained to remember at least one. Just when she thought she would not succeed, a scene surfaced from the abyss of her memory.

She clearly saw the front door of the apartment in which she lived. And not just that: she knew precisely in which building her apartment was, in which street the building lay. She remembered her address. But also something even more important. On the door was a small nameplate with the italicized letters *Bouvet*.

It made her want to slap her forehead. Bouvet, of course! Yet her relief did not last long. She had discovered, in fact, what her last name was, but not in which past. Was that her maiden name, or one that she had acquired through marriage? Which of her four husbands was named Bouvet: Thierry, Patrick, Claude or Jean-Marc? Which of her five lives awaited her behind the front door?

She strained once again, but there were no new scenes. What about looking at the pictures again? Maybe that would jog her memory. She raised the camera and quickly turned it back on. The screen glowed, but not a single picture appeared. Confused, she began pushing the buttons, but nothing changed, as if the camera's memory was empty.

She shrugged and put the camera back in her purse. This was, in fact, the best way. The trace of her other pasts now existed only in her memory. As it unavoidably grew weaker, those other lives would seem ever more like dreams. Beautiful and comforting dreams, even if they were strangely disturbing.

It was most important that along with them she should not nurse feelings of guilt. She had not chosen one of the five pasts, sacrificing the others. Someone else had retrieved the Bouvet surname from the dark lottery drum of her memory. God, chance or whatever, was it even important?

She had not the slightest inkling who would soon be waiting for her behind the front door. Whoever it was, she would be happy to see them. Still, she hoped it wouldn't be the fish.

7. The Sum

MR. ARNAUD MORIN—WHOM YOU see in the picture—hadn't sat down in the metro one single time over the course of the last eleven years. There might be an abundance of empty seats; he would remain standing just the same. That way, up on his feet, he got a good overview of the car, and it was thanks to this that he now noticed the unusual posture of the woman with the black leather purse who was sitting by the window just in front of him.

She first caught his attention when she suddenly rose and looked out at the station they were just leaving, as if she were seeking somebody on the platform. Then she turned toward the window as soon as the train entered the tunnel between stations and just stared at it, even though there was nothing to see outside. Next she looked for an extended period at some pictures on the screen of a small red camera, apparently surprised and pleased. Finally, even though there was no obvious reason, her hands began visibly to shake.

Mr. Morin, however, did not stand where he did because of the good view. It didn't mean much to him because he rarely paid attention to what was around him in the carriages of the metro. It wasn't clear to him why he had even noticed the woman in the light brown overcoat. He didn't usually take much interest in the antics of the other passengers.

He was on his feet in the metro because he thought best while standing. To be honest, he didn't resort to thinking very often. At work, for example, nothing of the sort was even expected of him. To the contrary. As a clerk in the military he was just supposed to follow regulations without delving into their meaning, viability or justification. There was no room for initiative or improvisation. In short, there was absolutely nothing for him to think about.

There was not much call for it at home either. His being a bachelor was a contributory factor. Marriage had never occurred to him, although he was already thirty-five, among other reasons because he feared a wife would introduce disorder into his life, which was organized according to the habits he'd acquired in the military schools he had attended since childhood.

He woke at six-fifteen (he had set the digital alarm clock to waken him to a trumpet call), made the bed for three and a half minutes (it took longer when he changed the sheets on Thursdays), did gymnastics for eighteen minutes (always naked to the waist, with the window open regardless of the temperature outside), attended to personal hygiene for twenty-three minutes (he undertook strict measures to be clean and orderly both at home and in public), made and ate breakfast (exclusively healthy, low-calorie, gluten-free food), checked whether everything in the apartment was in order (he knew it was, but still, just in case, a little precaution was called for, military personnel should be especially careful), and at a quarter to eight he set off for work. His shift did not begin before nine, and this was the surest way not to be late; even if all means of transport let him down, he could, if necessary, arrive on foot.

As he walked, he had a barely detectable limp in his right leg. He had injured it on maneuvers in his last year of military academy. At first it had seemed that amputation was unavoidable, but the doctors had somehow managed to save his leg, and afterwards his persistence and indefatigable spirit had contributed to his regaining almost full use of it. It felt like a rebirth when, after three and a half years of daily trips to the physical therapist, he was able to throw his cane away.

The injury, unfortunately, had signaled the end of his active service as an officer. Although he had a strong character, this briefly cast him into despondency; only gradually did he become convinced that he could still be quite useful in the background. The military administration actually needed people of his sort: conscientious, earnest, pedantic, dedicated, loyal, and above all not a thinker. He was proud of himself, and of the occasional praises of his superiors: only verbal ones so far, but one day there would be more tangible ones as well.

The time between returning from work and going to bed was also planned out. First he spent an hour and a half at the gym. His slightly less mobile leg did not stop him in any way from practicing karate; on the contrary, he managed to execute movements with it which others were unable to do.

After supper he would watch TV. He enjoyed watching sports and game shows. His favorite sports were handball and rugby, while he felt a certain disdain toward tennis and volleyball because there was no physical contact between the contestants. In terms of game shows, he thought he should try one himself, as it seemed to him that he knew more than many of the contestants, but he feared that stage fright might trip him up as it had during exams at the academy, bringing shame not so much on himself as on the army, and he dared not let that happen.

Before going to sleep he would always read for forty-five minutes. His favorite reading matter was history books, especially those about famous military leaders. He fancied himself as an adjutant who discreetly gave wise, victory-winning advice to some sort of generalissimo. He turned off the light at eleven exactly. If he did not sleep seven hours, he would not be up to the responsibilities that awaited him the next day.

Mr. Morin spent almost all of his free days outside of Paris. He believed it to be the duty of every patriotic Frenchman, and especially those in the armed forces, to get to know his country as well as possible. He composed a rather long list of places where military history had left the least tiny trace, and then set up a clear itinerary. He did not always return from his trips satisfied by the relationship of his countrymen toward their national past, but at least for himself he could say that he showed consistent respect toward French history.

If only he had found out in time that he was going to have Friday off, Mr. Morin could have already set off that day on the journey he had in prospect for the coming weekend. But he had only been told at the very end of yesterday that he was being rewarded with furlough, because the entire week before he had worked three hours' overtime daily in order to take care of an extraordinary and urgent job.

This time he was supposed to go by plane, and since he had bought the ticket for the lowest possible price, he could exchange it only by paying a rather large surcharge, which, thrifty as he was, he didn't really care to do, so he decided not to change his original plan. He would travel on Saturday and just see how to spend his free day in Paris.

By Friday morning he had planned only what he would do in the morning. He would indulge, as on every other working day, in his secret hobby. Later he would see what to do in the afternoon. If nothing else came to mind, he would visit the military museum. He went there once a month and he had already been this month, but he didn't really mind. He always felt good at the museum. He would spend the evening in his usual fashion.

His hobby didn't actually need to be a secret. There was nothing about it that was in conflict with Mr. Morin's service, and even less so with societal or moral norms. He considered it secret just because he had not reported it to military intelligence, which regularly handed out questionnaires to the administrative staff. The space for "your hobby" he left empty. If it were ever to be discovered that he actually was not without a hobby, and if they pressured him to expose not only what it was but why he kept it secret, he would have to admit: he was afraid of being ridiculed by some of his colleagues.

They also ridiculed him on the sly for a few other reasons, he knew that, but he paid no attention to them. He had long since forfeited the illusion that only the best Frenchmen were in the army. In it there were dishonorable, bad, even evil people, and most of all envious ones. Behind his back he was made fun of by those who envied his orderly life, his loyalty to his vocation, his idealism. Everything they themselves were not or did not possess.

If it were to become known that his hobby was doing math, someone would dig up the fact that he'd achieved barely passing grades in that subject at the military academy, and then they would even tease him openly about that. And were they to learn exactly which math problem interested him, their ridicule would have no end.

It was true, in fact, that mathematics had not been his best subject at the academy, but he didn't think that was entirely his fault. Professor Bonville shared part of the blame for it. He didn't know how to explain anything properly. He was a nervous and nasty man who easily lost patience if a student showed the least uncertainty. Who knew why, he had disliked Mr. Morin from the outset, to the point that he had even thought about giving up on his military studies at the end of the second year.

This, fortunately, didn't happen because Professor Bonville suddenly went on extended sick leave, and with Professor Lemercier, who replaced him, everything progressed more smoothly. In the first place, he was a better teacher, and even if Mr. Morin hadn't managed to improve his grade significantly, he did have the feeling that math was more accessible to him than before.

Old Professor Lemercier was the one who'd inspired Mr. Morin's hobby. From time to time he would digress during his lectures, and tell stories about mathematical topics beyond those being taught at the military academy. Once he cited a series of famous mathematical riddles which had driven many practitioners of this discipline to madness or even suicide.

Of all the problems the professor had mentioned, Mr. Morin and most of his colleagues were highly intrigued by Fermat's well-known last theorem. It had, in truth, recently been solved, but in a truly complicated way, not as simply as Fermat hinted that he had achieved, without leaving any clue. For a time, they argued fiercely about that mathematical ghost, only to have the excitement slowly die out when they remembered what inevitably awaited them if they continued in that direction.

In the end, even Mr. Morin cooled down, although it was he who most persistently dreamed of the fame awaiting him if he could only find Fermat's elegant proof. On top of everything else, that would be the best revenge on awful Professor Bonville, who would have to admit publicly how wrong he'd been about his ingenious student.

It was one winter afternoon during his long monotonous hours in physiotherapy that Mr. Morin remembered Professor Lemercier's old presentation on difficult mathematical problems. In the middle of an exercise where he was standing on his healthy leg, seemingly without reason, an older puzzle than Fermat's last theorem surfaced from his memory.

He probably would have forgotten it, like all the others, if it hadn't been accompanied by the professor's comment. He had mumbled it, as if talking to himself and not to his students. Mr. Morin would not have heard it at all if he hadn't been sitting in the first row.

"One has to have profound faith in order to solve that problem. . . ."

Neither in his student days nor later had Mr. Morin been interested in questions of religion, so he hadn't reflected on the meaning of the elderly professor's comment, but now, in the middle of physical therapy exercises, it started bothering him for some reason. Indeed, why must one believe, and deeply at that, to find an answer to the question of what the sum of all numbers is?

Even to him, who wasn't especially talented at math, it was clearly a fundamentally simple problem. Basic addition, nothing more complicated than that. Well, many numbers exist, and their sum cannot be quickly or easily calculated, but what did religion have to do with that? Why wouldn't there be a solution without it?

He would deal with this problem and show that, to solve it, it was enough to rely on reason, aided—because of the size of the task—by orderliness and persistence, the main principles of his life. Perhaps he was not good enough for something more intricate, but he certainly knew how to add. Perhaps mathematical fame awaited him after all.

Like every other job he took on, Mr. Morin approached this one systematically. He first asked from what position it would be best to go after the solution. It would never cross many people's minds, but as a man with military training, he knew that the path to victory generally led from a well-chosen attack position.

Immediately, he rejected lying down. What great mathematician had ever solved a problem stretched out in bed? To say the least, that would be undignified. What's more, if Mr. Morin was not reading, he got sleepy the moment he lay down.

Sitting was also not an option. Long ago he had acquired the conditioned reflex that he stopped thinking as soon as he sat down. That was the only way he could properly do his demanding job. However, it could hardly be that mathematics, even the most common stuff like addition, could be done without thinking.

The only choice that remained, therefore, was standing. Nothing simpler, one would say at first glance, but then unexpected problems cropped up. First of all, where should he stand? At work he certainly couldn't. There, even the two prescribed brief toilet breaks were frowned upon.

At home? Equally impossible. He would have to give something up for the sake of his hobby, and he wasn't happy about that. If only the thinking didn't last too long, he might manage to fit it in between two morning or evening activities in his schedule that he truly cared about. But great mathematical problems are not solved by dedicating just a few minutes a day to them.

On his trips? That was definitely not an option either. Should he stand for hours in front of historical monuments doing addition in his head? That would be trivializing, not honoring them.

Then came the question of how he should stand. He gave it a try and determined that he could not focus if he was walking or doing something while standing. He could think only if he was standing still.

He returned from physiotherapy on the metro feeling rather unhappy. So, it seemed that nothing would come of his mathematical hobby. He had no idea where and when he could stand still for at least an hour. With his left hand he held onto the stanchion, with his right he leaned on his cane. He would gladly have sat down, his exercises had worn him out, but there were no free seats because of the rush hour crowds.

Then, all at once, he realized that in fact, the lack of free seats was quite convenient. If he'd been sitting, he wouldn't have been thinking, so the obvious solution would never have come to him. The metro was actually the perfect place for his hobby. He spent at least an hour there every working day, and nothing prevented ed him from standing still and thinking. The carriage shook a bit and the passengers raised a clamor, but that was ignorable.

For the next eleven years, Mr. Morin rode the metro exclusively standing and never gave up searching for the sum of all numbers. It was uncertain how far he had got in his addition, because he managed to keep the whole thing secret. In the military intelligence records, he was still recorded as a clerk without a hobby. If he'd had any reason to speak of his progress, he would have said diplomatically that the problem was not yet solved, but that he was still full of enthusiasm to solve it.

His Friday off was a chance to think in the metro not in the usual manner, twice for half an hour as he went to work and back, but for a whole hour uninterrupted. He had never tried that. Who knew, perhaps it would prove itself more efficient; but only if he didn't get tired doing it. Sometimes even after half an hour he would get a headache from concentrating so hard.

He entered the carriage ready to get down to work, but then lost a quarter of an hour because he was distracted, quite unusually, by the strange posture of a woman with a black leather purse. Yet, fortunately, she had exited in the meantime, so that nothing stood in the way of his thinking process.

He had just drawn this conclusion when his office cell phone in the inside pocket of his jacket signaled that he had received a message.

Quickly pulling out the telephone, he thought that this could only mean one thing: something important had come up, his day off had been cancelled, he must go straight to work. He was in luck twice over. First, he had not already gone on his trip that day. If he had, he would have had to return with all speed to Paris from a great distance, and that certainly would not have been quick or cheap. Second, he was already in the metro so that in twenty minutes or so he would be at work, which would certainly impress his superiors.

Once his cell phone was in his hand, it occurred to him that it was unusual for them to contact him by SMS. In earlier emergencies, they had always called him. What had brought about this change? Had a state of war been declared, causing communications to switch to a special protocol?

As soon as he opened the message, it became clear to him that something worse than a state of war had occurred. Hackers had broken into military communications, even though they were considered the most highly protected. There was no text message, just a picture. He looked around to check whether anyone could see his telephone. Although he determined that no one could because everyone around him was sitting, he still raised it and held it closer, and then looked at the usual graphic representation of a hydrogen atom: a proton nucleus being circled by an electron.

He'd had no chance to ask himself what the meaning of this drawing was, when the picture changed, although he had touched nothing. On the screen, a spiral galaxy appeared. It stayed barely two seconds, then gave way to a sunset. The series went on at the same rate, allowing him no chance to find his wits. The sun was followed by a full moon scattered with craters, the blue and white Earth seen from outer space, the eye of a tornado interwoven with lightning, a whirlpool, a green apple, the yolk of a boiled egg, a brown iris, like his own.

Well, this was—as far as he was concerned at least— even worse than a hack into the military communications system, he said to himself as he stared at the final, tenth picture. The system probably wasn't in danger; only his cell phone was under attack. It wasn't difficult to figure out why he was the one chosen. One of the foreign intelligence services had discovered what it was that he did in secret.

It wasn't at all clear to him how they had managed to do so when no one had the slightest idea about his hobby, not even French intelligence, but at this moment that was the least important thing. They postulated that he was close to solving one of the greatest mathematical problems, and who knows what kind of military applications it might have. It might even lead to a completely new kind of weapon.

All at once the meaning of the photographs became clear. They seemed to be unconnected, but it was not so. Even while they were still appearing one after the other on the screen in front of him, he had recognized what it was that connected them. Something round appeared in them all. Now he understood that they were not just circles but zeros. Ten zeros. As many as there are in ten billion. It didn't matter what—euros, pounds, dollars. That was how much they were offering him for the solution.

He had real difficulty in preventing his hands from trembling, like the lady who until recently had been sitting by the window. Attempting to remain as inconspicuous as possible, he looked around the carriage. Who of the apparently harmless passengers was working for a foreign service? No one was looking in his direction, but that did not fool him. They certainly had their people near him, since they had decided to come out with their offer.

How mistaken they were about him. There were not

enough zeros in the cosmos to make Mr. Morin betray France. He was not like some of his colleagues who would do so for significantly less than ten. Now it was most important that he kept his wits about him. He must steal a chance to call French military intelligence agents to his aid. It would be best to pretend that he was looking through the pictures again, when actually he was sending an encoded call for help.

He had raised the phone slightly and put his thumb on the keyboard, when a strange sound echoed out. It was as if all the passengers in the carriage sighed harmoniously, loudly and deeply. He looked around again, expecting to see that others were also wondering what kind of intrusive sigh that was, but nobody else seemed to have heard it.

Then from somewhere deep in his memory recognition surfaced. That was exactly—though much more quietly, of course—how Professor Bonville would sigh when, while questioning young Mr. Morin, he would realize that his untalented student could not get something really simple into his head.

The next moment, the cell phone announced the arrival of a new SMS. It was surely a better offer, thought Mr. Morin, moving his thumb toward the button for opening messages.

Would it again be in pictures? And how many would there be now? This time, however, there were no images. Nor was there a text. Just three mathematical symbols:

$$\Sigma = 0$$

Mr. Morin stared at the symbols on the screen for a long time, unaware of the world around him. Finally, he returned the phone to his pocket, and then he did what he had avoided for the last eleven years in the metro: he sat down on the nearest empty seat. And he never got up again.

8. Halo

MRS. MADELEINE PRÉVOST—HERE SHE is in the picture—easily understood what was bothering the rather short gentleman who was now sitting two rows ahead of her, across the aisle. Seen from behind, his protruding ears and thinning hair were even more conspicuous, though he could not have been more than thirty-five years old.

She first spotted him because he remained standing, even though there were free seats nearby. Buried deep in thought, it was as if he didn't notice anything around him. Then he got a message on his telephone. He fearfully immersed himself in it. When another arrived soon after, he simply collapsed onto the nearest seat.

It wasn't hard to guess what had happened to him. When someone seems to have lost all hope—Mrs. Prévost knew very well—it must be love trouble. Nothing else can hit a man so hard. Doubtless his beloved had just announced that she was leaving him.

How terrible. Even someone as unattractive as this gentleman did not deserve to be left. Nobody deserved that. Love, however, is blind: people usually make the wrong choice and fall in love with those who will not return their affection. Is there anything more bitter than unrequited love? It is the leading cause of suicide.

Mrs Prévost's feeling of pity for the unknown gentleman quickly gave way to frustration. She was the only one who could help him at this difficult moment, but of course, he would never let that happen. He would not believe her. For that same reason, she had done nothing for the many others she could have and wanted to help over the last two and a half months.

Although she knew it was useless to do so, she took her cell phone from her purse. She didn't even try to conceal what she was doing, as she had in the beginning, when she was still quite hesitant. Neither then nor now did anyone notice her. She raised the phone and directed it at the back of the balding lop-eared man in front of her. Once she had taken his picture, she stared at it on the screen.

A surprise awaited her. He was supposed to have a halo of some color around his head, a fairly prominent one considering the state he was in, but there was nothing there. How could that be? Everyone she had taken pictures of till now had had what she called a love halo. Some smaller, some larger, but she had never seen anyone without any halo at all.

She was taken aback. Had the camera in her cell phone died perhaps? That would be a real catastrophe. There was no way she could have it repaired. What was she to tell the technical people—that her phone no longer captured halos? She quickly aimed it in a different direction. This time, the frame held three passengers. She was relieved when she saw from the new picture that the device was still working. All three had halos.

She once again observed from behind the gentleman without a halo. His troubles, it seemed, were not love related. He had no idea how lucky he was. Whatever else might be the problem, it would be easier for him.

On the other hand, he didn't know what he was missing out on by not being, as it seemed, touched by love. In spite of all the suffering it brings, how could anyone live without it? Indeed, what sort of a life was it for a man in which, as for this poor fellow, there was not a trace of love? Sighing, Mrs. Prévost prayed that she would never again take a picture of a person without a halo.

She had learned by pure accident late last summer that halos existed at all. Her old cell phone had gotten broken. She told Pierre that it had shut down and that she couldn't turn it back on. That was the truth, but not the whole of it. She kept from him that the problem was, in fact, the result of her clumsiness. If she had dropped it in some other place she would not have hesitated to tell him the whole story, but she didn't feel comfortable admitting to her son that it had fallen into the toilet, although he might have just smiled.

She tried to revive it, she wiped off the casing well, she even managed to open it by herself and dry the inside with a hair drier, but nothing helped. The telephone remained dead. Then she went to a shop in the neighborhood where they sold used cell phones. They had a lot of older models, but not as old as hers. They offered her a whole series of other, similar ones, at truly low prices, but she only wanted one exactly the same as hers so that Pierre wouldn't notice. When such a phone did not exist, she had to hide part of the truth from him.

She felt guilty because of that, although she did not lie to Pierre. The two of them were always completely honest with each other. She had repeated to him throughout his childhood, even too often perhaps, that honesty was extremely important. Even before Pierre was born, she had left his father because he was a dishonest man. This wasn't in fact the case, but as time went by she began believing herself the only lie she had ever told her son, which made it less than totally dishonest.

The father of her child had left her when he found out she was pregnant. That had been predictable, in fact. Her friends had warned her not to get into a relationship with him, that he would just seduce and then leave her as he had so many others, but she was convinced they were all just envious of her because of him. She was still young and naive, and he was enchantingly handsome. She fell in love like never before, and certainly like she never had since.

She tried to kill herself by taking more than half a bottle of sleeping pills, but someone saved her at the last moment. Then she decided to have an abortion, but she changed her mind in the waiting room. Not long after giving birth, she moved to another city and got a job, giving up on her studies. She dedicated her life completely to raising her son. She denied all other men access to her life.

A quarter of a century later, she experienced Pierre's marriage and move to another apartment as a second abandonment, although she didn't allow that to be seen. She understood it must be this way, but that didn't make it any easier for her. Fortunately, Pierre continued to live nearby and often visited her, alone or with Natalie, so she didn't feel too lonely.

At the end of one of his visits he surprised her. On his way out, he suddenly asked if she had ever thought about finding someone to live with.

"Someone?" she repeated in confusion.

"A man," he replied, "who is also alone."

"A man?" she was shocked.

"Or a woman, makes no difference," he added quickly. "Life is nicer with someone."

As soon as he had gone she burst into tears. How dared he even suggest something like that? She felt almost as betrayed as she had twenty-five years before. Was that the thanks she got for all she had done for him? She had dedicated her life to him, sacrificed everything for him, and he repaid her like this. No, that was not her Pierre, it couldn't be, that wife of his must have put him up to it. She was nice and caring while the three of them were together, but who knows what she filled his head with when they were alone. She was obviously jealous because Pierre often visited his mother; she wanted it to happen less frequently, perhaps even for him to stop seeing her altogether.

She cried for a long time that afternoon. In the evening, once she had calmed down a little, she asked herself what he'd really meant—to find herself a man? Even if she'd wanted to, and she didn't, was that so easy and simple? She had already gotten burned once by making the wrong choice—was she supposed to repeat the same mistake? True enough, this time she wouldn't get pregnant, but even so, she wouldn't be able to bear being left again. Even absolute loneliness was better than such a fate. Perhaps if she were sure that it wouldn't happen, that her choice would be the right one this time—but who could be certain of that? No one, of course. No, it just wasn't for her.

She expected Pierre to revert to the subject, so she thought of a reply—not too harsh, because it wasn't his fault, but still a reprimand, so that he would know he had hurt her feelings—but he never mentioned it again. She was actually contemplating whether she should initiate the conversation herself when the cell phone incident occurred.

Pierre was relieved at the news that her old phone no longer worked.

"Well, it was about time. How long have you had it—fifteen years?"

"Sixteen and a half."

"That must be a world record. Good, we'll get a new one right away."

"Can we find one just like this? Or a similar one? I've gotten used to it. . . ."

"They haven't produced that model for ages. And why would you want one? You can only make phone calls with it."

"Well, what are telephones for?"

He gave a little smile. "What aren't they for? Soon enough we'll be making cookies with them. You can, for example, take photos with a cell phone."

"I've already got a camera."

"This is more convenient. You don't have to carry both of them around. You have it all in one device."

"I very rarely take photographs."

"Whether you use it or not, every cell phone has a camera. And once you have it, maybe you'll use it more often than your camera."

"But what would I take pictures of?"

He did the smile again. "Well, the world. People. Life. Let your imagination run free and the inspiration will come."

When her son brought her the new phone, he barely spoke three sentences about the thing she was most interested in—how one made phone calls. She pretended to understand, even though she didn't. Once he had left, it took her a good half hour to teach herself how to use it. Her old phone had little keys, but everything on the new one was done on a touch screen.

Pierre had explained the camera at significant length. In great detail he explained how one took pictures, and everything about it was completely clear. She just had to get down to work. She did indeed get busy, not because she was overwhelmed with enthusiasm but because she wanted to make her son happy. She realized that, for some reason, he really wanted her to take pictures. And why not give it a try? Maybe she would start liking it eventually.

She awaited her son's next visit with a certain amount of discomfort. She knew that the first thing he would ask was whether she had taken any pictures. She would have loved to say that she hadn't, but lying wasn't an option, of course. Fine, what could she do: it would turn out that she hadn't really understood his explanations last time, because she was obviously doing something wrong. If she was doing it right, would all the people she photographed have a small colored halo around their heads? She must have missed some small detail or other, creating an effect like the red-eye phenomenon in older photographs taken with a flash. Pierre would tell her with a smile which setting was wrong, and there would be no halos in subsequent photos.

However, he ignored that completely. He praised her photos from the park. He really liked them. They were well-framed and well-lit. It was good that she had not stood facing the sun while she took them. She had an instinct for photography. She should certainly go on taking photos.

He's pretending not to see it, Mrs. Prévost concluded. He didn't want to criticize her so that she wouldn't get discouraged; he knew how sensitive she was. It would be better, however, if he told her where she was making the mistake, otherwise she would never free herself of these colorful halos.

"Something is not alright with the people. . . ." She offered him a chance to make mention of them after all.

He held the phone closer and looked more carefully at several photos with people in, then shook his head.

"I see what you mean. It's nothing. In the beginning, everyone slightly foreshortens the people they're photographing. You'll quickly learn how not to do that."

She was speechless for several moments, then took the phone back.

"I'd like to take your picture."

He gave a little smile. "Should I pose for you somehow?"

"This is just fine."

She snapped the photo from a short distance and then looked at it. The screen was filled with Pierre's head, framed by a thin dark green border. This could not be overlooked. She turned the phone toward her son.

His smile widened. "That's me."

She looked at him inquisitively. "You don't see anything unusual?"

He returned her inquisitive look. "What? You took a nice picture of me."

"Look closer."

He stared at the screen. "You mean how my face is a little bit distorted? It's always like that when you take a close up."

She knew no one as well as she did her own son. He was not pretending. He really didn't see the halo. For just an instant, she hesitated to tell him what she thought she saw on the photographs, then decided she would rather say nothing. Not at this time. There must be a problem with her vision. It could be nothing else. Pierre's was certainly all right. He would insist that they go straight to the ophthalmologist, and she was disgusted by doctors. All of them. From back at the time of the abortion that never happened.

And anyway, in the strictest sense, she had no reason to visit an ophthalmologist. What she had was not damaged eyesight, but an improved one. She wasn't seeing less, but more. Why couldn't it just stay that way? Better that than for a bunch of doctors to harass her, for whom she would be just another medical case. A guinea pig.

As soon as Pierre left, she got down to studying the photographs she had taken the day before yesterday in the park. The halo could be especially well seen in two of them. She had photographed two couples, one young, the other older. She had not worried that they would notice her. She stood off to the side, at a good distance, and they were preoccupied with themselves, though in different ways. The young couple was kissing, the elderly pair were having a heated argument.

Only now did she notice something she had missed earlier, even though it was quite noticeable. The young people had halos of almost the same color. Their heads were touching as they kissed, so it looked like they were surrounded by a single light blue frame. The elderly couple, however, had halos of quite different colors: hers was cherry-red, and his was ochre.

Then she got an idea. She quickly looked through the photos once again, but there weren't any more couples in them. She made a sudden decision which was inconsistent with her restrained character: she would go out straight away and take more pictures of couples. That was the only way to check if her supposition was correct.

She returned to the park and took up a position on a bench, holding the cell phone ready to shoot. It was a sunny day, the place was busy, but for a full forty minutes, as if out of spite, not a single couple came by. She would have to go somewhere else, somewhere where there were more people. She thought about it, then headed for the nearest metro station. It was a small one, true, but she would travel to the closest large one. It was almost always crowded there, and there would be bound to be some couples, too.

It turned out that the crowd was too big. Even though there were couples, it wasn't easy to photograph them. Someone always got in the way. She thought about it some more. It would be best to ride the rails for a while. It was crowded in the carriages, but people moved around less than at the station so she would have more opportunity to take pictures.

And she really did, but then a new problem arose. Whenever she wanted to take a photo, she would be overcome with discomfort. It seemed to her that the passengers were looking at her with disdain. She missed five or six couples because she ashamedly lowered the hand with the phone before taking the shot. She rode for at least an hour and a half before this fear subsided. She realized that actually no one was paying any attention to her, and if someone happened to observe her they would think that she was, in fact, taking a selfie, and that would be strange to no one. People were constantly doing that, as she had discovered as she watched those around her.

She spent more than two and a half hours on the

metro, but it paid off. She photographed as many as ten couples. It was more than enough to confirm her idea. Seven couples had the same or quite similar halos, which meant that they were made for one another. For the rest, the halos were different, and thus, inevitably, those relationships would be short-lived. Three of those six would soon be abandoned, and then a suffering awaited them which Mrs. Prévost knew from her own experience to be terrible.

As she was returning home, a thought occurred to her. If she had had this cell phone a quarter of a century ago and known about the halos, her life would have turned out differently. She would have taken a picture of Pierre's father and herself and easily established what kind of future awaited them, and she would have avoided the relationship with him. Or maybe she wouldn't? Would even such hard evidence be enough to bring her to her senses? It was hard to say. Love was not only blind, but deaf as well. She'd been too much in love to be influenced even by the most convincing voice of reason. Moreover, if it hadn't been for the relationship with Pierre's father, there would be no Pierre. She was horrified at the thought, so she quickly banished it from her mind.

In any case, it was too late for her, but not yet for Pierre. If he was in danger of the same fate, she could still undertake measures. To warn him, if nothing else. On the surface, he and Natalie loved each other, everything appeared harmonious between them, but that could be just an illusion. What people concealed in their minds was unknown. Or rather, it had been unknown before the halos appeared. Now one picture would be enough to establish what was really going on.

She didn't have the patience to wait for their next

visit, so she invited them over. She would make the cookies they both loved. Pierre saw nothing unusual in that. From time to time she would do so when she longed for company. There was also nothing strange in her suggestion—once they had arrived—that she take their picture. He had told Natalie about his mother's new hobby. The daughter-in-law, of course, had nothing against it, she just complained that she wasn't looking her best, she would have dressed up a little if she had known they were going to have their picture taken.

Mrs. Prévost was relieved when she saw in the picture that the two halos were almost the same color. Fate had spared her son the destiny intended for his mother. Pierre and Natalie understood her smile as an expression of satisfaction by a photographer with a job well done.

Then he suggested that he take his mother's picture. At first she objected for the same reason as Natalie. She was not dressed for it. However, Pierre responded that she could always just erase the photograph if she didn't like it. That left her with no excuse. She straightened her hair and clothes, then struck a rather stiff pose.

Her son and his wife announced that it had come out really well, but she paid no attention to that. She was only interested in the halo. A lump rose to her throat. She looked for a moment at the previous picture, though she didn't need to. Even without the comparison it was immediately clear to her that her son's halo was quite a different color from hers.

Pierre, so it seemed, did not love her at all. There was only room in his heart for Natalie. But that was not possible. She might have been deceived by other men, but surely not by her own son. Among other things, he was constantly demonstrating love for her, taking care of her, he was dedicated and attentive to her. No, something else was afoot in this case. And then she realized what it was. The halos were related to just one kind of love: the romantic kind, not that between a mother and son or someone else. This time she let out an audible sigh as she smiled anew.

"I knew you would like it," Pierre said. "I'm not such a bad photographer myself."

Mrs. Prévost went on photographing couples in the metro at least twice a week. She was happy to find halos of the same color, as most of them were, but she was saddened by the less frequent encounters with differing colors. She quickly became convinced that she could foresee how couples with different colored halos would break up. The ones with darker shades would leave those with lighter ones. She imagined that there would be significantly more women among the abandoned, but it turned out that there were almost as many men.

She would gladly have helped both men and women to avoid their horrible fate, but how could she go about it? Could she just walk up to them and warn them of what awaited them? They would think she had lost her mind. It would do no good to show them the photograph, where it could easily be seen, since they would be blind to the obvious, just as Pierre and Natalie had been.

As a result, she became so frustrated that she decided not to photograph couples anymore. Of what use were the pictures if they could not help anyone? She was getting upset for nothing. For a while she quit going to the metro altogether, but she missed more and more the photographs of halos which only she could see, until she changed her mind. She returned to her passion, now photographing individuals.

It turned out, however, that this also caused frustration. Once she had taken pictures of about a hundred passengers in the metro, it became evident to her that among them were many halos of a quite similar nuance. If they could somehow get into a relationship, they would be almost perfect couples. Unfortunately, their life paths did not cross. They passed each other by, unaware of what they were missing. Mrs. Prévost could have revealed to them their ideal partners, she had proof of it, but again, no one would believe her.

The photo of the man without any kind of halo was the last straw. The built-up frustration turned to anger. This damned telephone was to be blamed for it all. If it weren't for that, her life would be a lot easier. Why did she need any of this? She was behaving like a crazy old woman, spending hours in the metro, clandestinely taking pictures of strangers, imagining that she saw some sort of halos, desiring to get mired in the lives of others.

She would exit at the next station, drop the cell phone into the closest trash can, and upon returning home she would stop by that shop with used phones and buy the plainest one available. Definitely without a camera. If Pierre was interested in taking pictures, let him do so till the cows came home. She had had more than enough.

She stood up and only then noticed a person whom she had not seen behind the big-eared and balding passenger, who now sat as if he intended to stay there forever. The refined, elegantly dressed gentleman was perhaps a year or two older than she, with symmetrical facial lines, gray but still thick hair, prominent eyebrows. Though he wasn't standing, it was evident that he was tall. In his lap he had a closed crimson book.

Mrs. Prévost then did something, even though she was aware that it made no sense whatsoever. In a minute or two she would be free forever of this cell phone, so why would she bother to take one more picture? She hushed that reasonable question in herself, raised the phone and snapped the shot.

She immediately realized that the unknown gentleman had a special halo, but she had to strain to figure out what was so special about it. When it did flash into her mind, she feverishly began looking for one other special picture among the multitude of ordinary ones: for the only photograph in her cell phone that she had not taken herself.

She looked at the border around her own face in Pierre's picture, then quickly returned to the latest picture and focused on that same detail. She had not been wrong. She had already come across halos of a similar colour to hers, but she had never seen such a complete match of nuance.

What now? Her muffled frustration was again aroused. Her helplessness to do anything about it hit her like physical pain, so that for a moment she completely cramped up. As if that suffering were not enough, the train began slowing, and the dashing gentleman got up and went to the nearby door.

When the doors opened, something snapped inside Mrs. Prévost. She must go after him. She would catch up to him, stop him and tell him everything. Stuttering, clumsy, confusing. Why should she care if he didn't understand, if he thought she'd lost her mind, if he turned his back on her and left? She would be able to live with that. It wouldn't be the first time a man had turned his back on her. But if she went on just standing there, if she didn't take action, no matter how crazy it all seemed, she would never be able to forgive herself.

She stepped off the train at the moment the doors started to close.

9. The Agent

AGENT ALFRED LEROUX-VIDAL—WHOM YOU see in the picture—would always enter the metro carriage walking backwards. It was a safety measure of vital importance in his job. Weren't there already so many secret agents who'd died at that very same spot? It was difficult to defend oneself when attacked from behind in a huge crowd, and the attacker would as a rule remain unnoticed.

Whenever he had to ride the metro, agent Leroux-Vidal tended to board at the smallest stations, with as few passengers as possible. He preferred it when nobody else entered or left the carriage through the same door as he, although not even then would he feel completely safe. He could always get hurt from a distance. There was no hundred per cent reliable protection in this vocation. One way or another, a secret agent's life was always in danger.

While entering the carriage backwards protected him from an exterior attack, it made him more exposed to an attack from the interior. One of his colleagues often made a banal jest that wherever one stood, one's back was always in the back. He ended up with a bayonet stuck under his shoulder blade. The long blade first ran through a not particularly thin partition he was leaning against in the toilet of a theater, convinced that nobody could do him any harm.

When someone brushed up against agent Leroux-Vidal on this occasion as he was boarding the metro backwards, at first he was sure it was an attack. He cringed instinctively, expecting the worst, but nothing happened. Past him went a middle-aged woman who, as it seemed, had decided to get off at the last moment. The door closed the second she stepped onto the platform. For as long as the train was leaving the stop he didn't take his eyes off her. She didn't turn around even once, as if she were a completely innocent passenger, but that is exactly how every professional would behave. She had tried to off him, for some reason she hadn't managed to do so, and now she was inconspicuously getting away. Until next time.

When the train entered a tunnel, agent Leroux-Vidal turned around and out of habit first carefully examined his surroundings. He had a photographic memory, which had more than once saved his life. If he closed his eyes, behind his eyelids a clear image of the inside of the carriage would appear. However, he did not do that. It would have been reckless. Although everything looked safe at first glance, it could easily have been an illusion.

Moving nimbly, ready to jump aside in case of a threat, he headed toward the back of the carriage. This time he was lucky. The seat which suited him most was available—in the left corner across from the exit and entrance door while the train was going in that direction. Nobody could hurt him from behind there. The wall behind him was made of metal, and was therefore impenetrable even to the sharpest bayonet. (High-caliber ammunition would doubtless pierce it, but certain risks had to be accepted.) The place also offered an excellent view of the half-empty carriage. No one would have time to attack him from the front without being spotted.

Agent Leroux-Vidal finally had a chance to relax. From his barely audible sigh one might have supposed that he found his calling quite difficult. After all, what pleasure could he possibly find in the constant stress, tension and fear that someone was out to kill him?

The answer was the following: he was an adrenalin addict. After years of living on the edge he could no longer do without the sheer thrill of it. The one thing he dreaded more than his daily roster of perils was the day of his retirement, when his dose of adrenalin would no longer be available. Deep inside he nursed the morbid hope that death would solve this problem before retirement came.

There were other, more innocent elements of an agent's role on which he had also become dependent. Like identity change, for example. Agent Alfred Leroux-Vidal's name wasn't actually Leroux-Vidal—that is, it was, but only on Fridays. Tomorrow he would be somebody else, just as he'd been a different person the day before. Every day of the week he had a different name, or rather, a different identity. To ordinary mortals even two identities would be too difficult to cope with, but he was able to handle seven without breaking a sweat, and even enjoy it. He was in a quandary as to whether he would return to his original identity if he lived long enough to retire. Over time he'd become rather fond of assuming other identities.

The train was just arriving at another stop when agent Leroux-Vidal heard a message alert coming from one of his numerous pockets. He had seven phones on him, one for each identity. He didn't have to carry them all because it was inconceivable that one of them should ring on the wrong day. Yet he still took them everywhere with him, on the grounds that that was where they were safest. No matter how well he hid the phones, there was always the chance his enemies might get their hands on them, in which case his only option would be to commit suicide. This way they could only seize the phones if they killed him first, but then they would be of no possible use.

Now the inconceivable actually happened. A ringtone informed agent Leroux-Vidal that he had received an SMS on the cell phone he used exclusively on Mondays. That was a red alert signal. Lightning fast, he changed from being slightly relaxed to being fully alert, as previously.

Grasping it between his thumb and index finger, he removed the phone from his jacket pocket. He did it imperceptibly, as if he were picking his own pocket. He kept it concealed in his large hand, constantly looking down the carriage. Three doors had just opened. When they closed a minute later, he knew precisely how many passengers had left, and how many had entered the carriage. By the time the train dived into a new tunnel, he'd managed to examine the newcomers carefully. They all stood some distance from him, but that didn't make them any less suspicious. He would keep a surreptitious eye on them.

He tapped the smooth surface of his phone several times without looking. The message was probably supposed to distract him. He only had time to look at the screen for an instant. But even that would be enough. There was no match for him when it came to speed reading. However, nothing was there to be read. Instead of text, he'd received a picture. He was so taken aback that he remained engrossed in it twice as long as he knew he should. Fortunately, nobody tried to take advantage of his momentary distraction.

He'd been photographed from the front while entering the carriage backwards. The woman who'd brushed up against him was also in the photograph. She was stepping onto the platform, so he was now able to see her face. This could mean either that she was indeed a regular passenger or that those responsible for all this wanted to make him believe she was.

He didn't have to guess what was going on. He'd been exposed, through no one's fault but his own, because that never happened to people who did their job impeccably. He didn't know, however, where he'd made a mistake, but he must have made one somewhere. If he hadn't, how else could they have found out that he would be on the metro at this time? How had they gotten the number of the phone he used on Mondays? How had they photographed him when he remembered clearly that after him nobody else had remained on the platform who could have done it?

It was useless, however, to rack his brains with these questions now. He'd been exposed and he had to accept it. The fact that he was still alive was encouraging. Had they wanted to assassinate him, they wouldn't have had any problem. They could also have aimed something more deadly than a camera at him. Since they hadn't, it meant that they needed him alive. Therefore, they would contact him again. Soon, probably.

There was no point in attempting anything in the meantime. He was basically trapped. Who knew how many so-called passengers had their eyes fixed on him, although it seemed like nobody was paying him any attention. He wouldn't even manage to get up, let alone reach the door and rush out at the next stop. At this point it was most important to keep his presence of mind and not act rashly.

Another message arrived as they were entering the station. The second message alert, however, did not come from the phone in agent Leroux-Vidal's hand, but again from one of his pockets. The phone for Tuesdays—his trained ears recognized the sound. For a second he wasn't sure if he should put the one for Mondays back in its pocket, but he left it in his lap instead. What was the point of hiding something that was already revealed? Then he reached for the other phone.

Again, he received a picture and yet again he was in it, this time on his own. He'd been photographed just a few moments earlier, when he'd already taken out the first phone. It looked as if the photographer were standing in front of him, only two or three steps away. However, there had been nobody at that spot. The photographer must therefore have been somewhere further away, perhaps even at the other end of the carriage, and zoomed in multiple times.

He quickly looked around at the passengers and examined them. Five of them were holding cell phones, none of which was aimed at him. That didn't mean anything. His seven cell phones could also take pictures from any angle. Only one other passenger was holding something else in his hands: a man in a red sweater, who was sitting at the opposite end of the car. Ever since agent Leroux-Vidal had entered the carriage, the elderly gentleman hadn't taken his eyes off what seemed to be a book he was reading, but it didn't necessarily have to be that at all.

And besides, it didn't really matter who had photographed him and from where. The new message only emphasized what he'd already been told in the first.

His life was in their hands, any form of resistance was futile, it was best to cooperate. That probably wouldn't save his life—exposed agents shouldn't count on longevity—but it might spare him needless suffering.

In fact, he was already prepared to escape torture. The moment he'd realized something odd had been going on, he'd executed the imperative instructions: with the tip of his tongue he removed the cap from the top of his lower left molar. Now all he needed to do was to bite through the capsule inserted in the hole in his tooth, and he would die instantly. He still hadn't done that, not because he was a coward, but because there was no reason to be hasty. There was always time for that move. He would first see what his enemies were planning to do with him.

He'd already guessed when and where the next message would come. It was always more convenient to deal with people who followed a certain pattern. As soon as the train began to slow down ready for the next stop, he put the cell phone for Tuesdays on his lap too, and then stuck his hand in the pocket holding the phone for Wednesdays. That very instant he heard a third SMS alert. He expected it to contain another picture, and that once again he would be in it, but he couldn't even begin to imagine where on the metro he'd been photographed this time.

However, as it turned out, they weren't entirely predictable. Yes, it was a picture and he really was in it, but not on the metro. At first he was uncertain of his whereabouts. For a few long seconds he stared at his naked body in the shower before recognizing by the details that he'd been photographed in the bathroom of the apartment he used on Fridays.

Just as with the cell phones, each one of his identities

went with its own apartment. The photograph could have been taken on a previous Friday, but it had more probably been taken that morning. If they had photographed him earlier, why would they have delayed their scheme? In this profession, too, you strike while the iron is hot.

The situation was worse than he'd thought. Not only had they managed to trace him and find out his phone numbers, but they'd also got into his safe house. He had no idea how they'd succeeded in that. The apartment for Fridays was located in the garage unit of a building, on the second subterranean floor, and had a camouflaged entrance door. For entering and exiting he used passages, mostly through the sewer, that led to the neighboring public buildings. There was no way he could be followed down there because the whole place was covered with sensors.

The apartment itself was well-equipped with various electronic devices. The security systems would react even to the most subtle movements, and there were also infrared cameras which were constantly recording. Moreover, for as long as he was there, he was completely shut off from the rest of the world. At the entrance he took the cards and batteries out of all his cell phones, plus he had no internet connection or any other form of communication, so there was nothing for them to monitor.

Yet still, not only had they overcome all the obstacles he'd set for them, but they'd also photographed him in this utterly undignified pose. The intention behind it was twofold: to show him they were the ones in control, as well as to humiliate him. Whatever the dénouement, his professional reputation was destroyed. Who would ever take seriously an agent who'd been photographed bare-bottomed in the place he naively considered safest?

Furthermore, although it may not have been true, he had now to suspect that the other six apartments had been broken into as well. Even if by some miracle he slipped out of this trap, he would have nowhere else to go. That meant that all the operations he was engaged in under various identities were to be temporarily or permanently aborted, and that he must become a sleeper, for an extensive period, by the looks of it.

The only fortunate circumstance out of his misfortune was that he wasn't keeping anything in any of his apartments that would put the agency he worked for in danger. He hadn't imperiled any of his colleagues' lives. He was the only one suffering, and as long as that was the case, however unpleasant it was going to be for him, the damage would be minimal. Somebody had invested enormous effort into kicking him out of the game and they had succeeded, but if they'd been hoping to catch bigger prey, they had another thing coming.

Perhaps they were actually still hoping to. They thought they had him cornered, and that eventually he would tell them everything they wanted to know. New photographs were surely on their way. However, what could be in them? They had nothing else to blackmail him with. They'd destroyed his career as an agent, he didn't have anything else to lose, so he wasn't going to tell them anything, and if they tried to force him, there was always the capsule.

The reception of another SMS once again coincided with the train's entering the station. Agent Leroux-Vidal added a third cell phone to the first two. Up until just fifteen minutes earlier such a scene would have seemed unbelievable to him. What agent would attract other people's attention by piling up cell phones in his lap? He, however, already considered himself a former agent, so he was no longer obliged to care about remaining inconspicuous.

The photograph on the screen of the phone for Thursdays was different from the other three. For the first time, he wasn't in it. Instead, there was a boy, about nine years old. Skinny, with freckled skin and unruly red hair, dressed in shorts and a muddy long-sleeved shirt, on a grass-covered playground, his foot resting on a football.

Agent Leroux-Vidal was proud of his expressionless face. Not even in the most tense situations was one able to tell what he was thinking or feeling. Had he been a poker player, this would certainly have been a great advantage. Now, however, his unreadable face momentarily formed a grimace of pain and powerlessness. He didn't even try to pull himself together, although he was aware that he was being closely watched, and surely being recorded.

He knew well that nothing was deemed holy in his profession. To achieve a goal, any line could be crossed or consideration disregarded, any commitment, promise or oath broken. It was a world without honor, where everything was allowed.

Still, there was a single taboo which—as far as he knew—nobody had violated yet. The one and only holy thing: agents' children. Whatever the circumstances, on no account had they ever been involved in ongoing affairs, nor had anyone tried to use them as a means of achieving an objective. Not ever—until now.

Whenever he observed his own life with the eyes of an agent—which was mostly the case—it was the biggest mistake he'd ever made. Everything had spoken against that relationship: the voice of reason, the strict service regulations, the non-existence of a future. But has love ever cared about such obstacles?

She too had been an agent. Fortunately, she'd worked for the same agency, so at least the issue of treason had never been brought up. She hadn't been supposed to get pregnant, and when she had, she hadn't been allowed to give birth. All of it would have been kept a secret had she aborted—although unpleasant, it was a routine procedure, and such acts of carelessness did occasionally happen—but she hadn't. And so the inevitable had happened. She had been dismissed from the service, and he had been demoted to a rookie position.

A year after she'd given birth, she'd been found dead. It had been concluded in the investigation that she had probably been assassinated by an enemy agency. Since she'd refused to be under total protection, they'd used the opportunity to get back at her for something big she did against them. He'd been forced to accept the official explanation, although he'd suspected that there could have been other motives behind the murder as well. Such as, for example, the fact that she'd known too much. However, he couldn't prove anything; and even if he could, he wouldn't know what to do with the proof. How could he declare war on his own agency?

The child had been put up for adoption, and he had been strictly forbidden from establishing any contact with his son, even seeing him from a distance. He'd respected that rule for almost five years as he'd been working his way up to his former position. Only after he'd regained it, and with it the privilege of unmonitored movement, had he gone in absolute secrecy to the place where the little boy lived. (It had taken a lot of skill and blackmail to find out his address.)

He'd only seen him briefly, while the boy had been playing football with friends on the very same playground shown in the photograph that had been sent to his fourth cell phone. He wouldn't have recognized him among the other boys had he not had his mother's facial features. The father had feared the excitement which had overwhelmed him as he'd watched his son through binoculars from the edge of a tiny wood. He must not come here again, he'd decided. At least not while still on active service. The following three years he'd been managing, as a good agent, to resist the temptation, even though at times it had gotten highly intense.

He figured out right away why his son's picture had been sent to him. It was meant to take away his privilege of committing suicide. As long as he'd thought that nobody knew about the boy, he'd been more than ready to kill himself if they pushed him too far. The capsule in the tooth was no secret. All agents had a trump card of the sort and were ready to play it if left no other choice. However, now they'd let him know that by sentencing himself, he would also be sentencing his own son to death. The last taboo had been violated, and he'd been denied the ultimate choice. He had to cooperate.

Something else was also puzzling, and not in the least less unpleasant than this extortion. How had they learned about the boy in the first place, or rather, how had they found out his whereabouts? Only the agency leaders had been informed of the first matter, and about the latter, not even they knew, only the independent protection agency. To discover these two secrets, not one, but two moles were necessary. And something like that was simply unthinkable, because it would mean that. . .

Agent Leroux-Vidal had no time to prognosticate all the consequences of the unthinkable because the train was arriving at the next station, which was accompanied by a new message—sent to the phone for Fridays, as predicted. When the fourth phone also ended up in his lap, the people around him no longer looked at him merely surreptitiously, but he did not care about that at all.

For the first time, it was a group photograph. At a round white table, seven persons were sitting on white wooden chairs: three young women, three young men, and an elderly gentleman. They were located in a round windowless room. There was no other furniture, no decorations or carpets. Only blank walls, a bare floor and a low ceiling. Everything was white. Even the clothes the people were wearing were white: the overalls, caps and gloves.

He was perfectly familiar with everything he saw in the picture. And how could he not be—he was one of the three young men. For years, he had regularly attended the briefings held once a month in the dead room—the only place in the world where they could safely share information which was in no way meant to be heard by the wrong people. It was where Daddy—the head of the agency—revealed his innermost secrets.

His face was hidden behind a white mask, even in the presence of his closest colleagues. To them, he was just an elderly man's voice that was never raised. The incontestable voice of the one pulling all the strings in the greatest of games, the one who often decided who lived and who died. As far as they knew, he remained invisible even to the president and the prime minister. Only one man was entitled to see him without the mask: the Minister of Internal Affairs.

Security in the dead room was maintained via the strictest of precautions. In order to enter it, one had to take off all one's clothes, go through no fewer than three scan checks, then put on overalls, gloves and a cap to cover one's hair. No object whatsoever could be brought into the room.

How the camera had ended up in there and how the picture had been imperceptibly taken, he could not even begin to imagine. It required not just a mole, but a true wizard, or at least a magician, to pull off something like that. The whole team had been sitting at that table, only the top agents, and they'd all let themselves be outsmarted by a traitor in their midst. They'd turned out to be more naive than children; the only thing missing had been for the impostor to shout: "Say cheese!"

The damage was immeasurable. Even if there hadn't been an audio recording—and it was better to count on it: sound was recorded more easily than images—this photograph was enough to injure the agency irreparably: all its main operatives were put on view like on a wanted list; the only thing left to do was for someone to announce the beginning of the hunt.

Completely oblivious to his surroundings in the metro carriage, he lifted the fifth phone slightly and began to scan the faces of those at the round table. Although he knew that in his profession one was never to trust anyone unconditionally, he couldn't turn suspicious against any of his five fellow agents. That would be like being suspicious of himself. But still, somebody had to be the mole.

As a response to this particular thought, in his pock-

et the cell phone for Saturdays sounded the SMS signal. For the first time the pattern was broken. The next
stop was nowhere near; they were in the middle of a
tunnel. Earlier on, he'd been able to hide his excitement, but now he simply did not care. He just put the
fifth phone on top of the other ones lying in his lap,
then feverishly reached for the sixth.

He looked fixedly at the photograph of an unfamiliar
man shown in the new picture. He could only see his
head. The man was approximately seventy, had grayish
hair, a neat mustache, a small double chin, thick side-
burns and a round face. There was something amiable
about his expression. If he were an actor, he certainly
wouldn't fit the role of a bad guy.

Just as he wouldn't be the right person for the role of
leader of a powerful secret agency, thought agent Leroux-Vidal, wide-eyed when he realized who was in the
photograph. Had he run into this old man somewhere,
nothing would have been further from his mind than
to suspect that he was Daddy, but perhaps that was the
way it was supposed to be. As if his position could have
been held by someone whose appearance instantly gave
away what he did for a living!

However, what good was that at this point, when
it had been discovered anyway whose face it was behind the white mask? It was an absolute catastrophe.
Not only were the lead operatives unveiled, but also the
head of the agency. There was nothing left to save, they
would have to shut down and then start over, with new
members. Which would in no way be simple and it
would take months, even years, before everything was
up and running, and in the meantime the state would
be left practically wide open to the numerous threats to
its security. What an utter disaster.

But before stepping down, the old operatives must complete one more task, in any way possible and at any cost. No sacrifice was too great. They had to find out the identity of the mole. If not, a shadow would remain over the agency's future, a constant fear of the traitor who'd be enjoying his freedom, who'd have exceptional authority and who would be able to strike hard again.

Immersed in such thoughts of panic, agent Leroux-Vidal had failed to notice that in the meantime the train had stopped at yet another station, that nine passengers had left, and six had gotten on. None of that was important to him any longer. His absent-mindedness ceased when, in the next tunnel, he heard a message alert coming from the last cell phone, the seventh, which he used to use on Sundays.

As he was looking for room on his lap for his sixth phone, he decided to put them all back into their pockets as soon as he saw the new picture. Not because the passengers around him were now obviously staring at him, some even filming him. Even that was of no concern. He was going to put them back because he felt encumbered, and had a growing desire to escape.

He was convinced that this time too they'd sent him a picture. There is reason behind the saying that a picture is worth a thousand words. All the pictures he'd gotten so far were very eloquent, so he'd had no other choice but to believe in what they'd been telling him. What else was there to be told through a picture? Hadn't everything already been said? The whole agency was faced with ruination.

Perhaps they were going to introduce themselves finally? Look, we are the ones who destroyed you. We feel so confident that we do not hesitate to show ourselves. You will never find out who our guy is, and he will become active again as soon as you reestablish your agency.

He tapped the screen of the seventh phone with shaking fingers. The picture showed a park bench. Painted green, it blended into the rich vegetation in the background. At each end there sat a young man and an elderly woman, both preoccupied with the same activity: browsing through their cell phones.

She could have been about sixty-five; she had soft facial features, hair that was still thick, and large-framed glasses. The affable old woman was smiling because of something she could see on the screen of her phone, which also made her dimples show. He was about thirty-five, seemed tall, had a long face and large hands. His facial expression was full of tension, as if he were being particularly careful not to make a mistake in what he was doing on the phone.

Agent Leroux-Vidal pushed the seventh phone away as if what he held his hands were suddenly red hot. The phone first fell on top of the other ones on his lap, and then slid off onto the floor of the carriage. He remained petrified for a moment. Then he began shaking his head in disbelief.

This was not true. It couldn't be. He'd never sat on that bench, he had no idea whatsoever where that was. Neither had he ever seen that woman before. The man only looked like him, it wasn't him. Or it was digitally altered; it didn't matter. He was not the mole; they were putting all the blame on him so as to hide the real traitor. What was he supposed to do now?

The answer to this question was sevenfold. All the phones rang at the same time. He jumped up instantaneously, and the six phones in his lap also ended up on the floor. The urge to escape overshadowed everything else. He rushed through the carriage, disregarding the fact that he was stepping on his phones, bumping into passengers, being recorded from every angle.

He headed for the door while the train was still moving. Somebody attempted to calm him down, but he pushed them away. He was trying insanely hard to pry the door open until, upon stopping at the station, it opened by itself. He stormed out, but at that very moment he realized he'd made a fatal mistake. He should have gotten off backwards, the way he'd gotten on.

10. The Image Interpreter

~ I ~

MISS MARGOT VERDIER you do not see in the picture. Not because she is invisible, but unnoticeable. A multitude of people had ridden with her that November Friday in the same carriage of the metro, and yet no one had seen her. She had entered their field of vision, but it was as if she hadn't been there. She melted into the impersonal background like a seat or a window, giving no one a reason even to notice, much less remember her. Upon leaving the metro, who would remember the seat on which they had sat or the window they had been next to, if they had not been unusual in some way?

Nature was partly to be blamed for the unremarkable appearance of Miss Verdier, but she was also somewhat responsible. Nature had graced her with ordinariness in all things: height, stature, but above all her face. She was neither pretty nor ugly—a real nightmare for a writer to describe. In truth, how does one describe someone's countenance if they are so commonplace that they neither attract nor repulse you? In literature, it is a well-known fact that average faces are hopelessly difficult to put into words, as opposed to beautiful or hideous ones, about which there is plenty to say.

It was as if Miss Verdier was making a special effort to emphasize this plainness of hers. She used no makeup whatsoever, so she looked pale, almost ill. She had straight hair which she didn't even try to improve with a hairstyle. She simply let it grow, cutting it when it reached three fingerwidths above her shoulders. Her clothing was even worse. There was nothing fashionable about what she wore, a classic style, which added at least ten years to her age; also, it was as if she was trying to choose the most colorless of colors. Her shoes completed the picture, being more suited to a woman nearing retirement than one who was yet to turn forty.

While it was not strange that Miss Verdier went unnoticed, it was harder to explain why she was not in a single photograph taken in the carriage on that exceptional morning when, by a confluence of circumstances, dozens of pictures were taken from a variety of angles. The passenger sitting on the folding seat across from the middle door was nowhere to be found in them, as if all the cell phones and cameras had also remained blind to her unremarkable presence.

This was even stranger, because Miss Verdier did not stick in one place. That would, after all, have been too much, since she spent more than four hours in the metro. Occasionally she would stand up so that she herself could take photos of a passenger who caught her interest. However, it so happened that no one else was taking photos at those moments, so the opportunity for her also to be immortalized was lost.

Miss Verdier was not only aware of the fact that people didn't pay heed to her, she even counted on it. When she saw someone interesting, she would approach them without hesitation and take a close-up. She knew she would not attract their attention. It happened thus as many as nine times that Friday, even though you'd expect at least some of those people to notice, since it was neither convenient nor pleasant for them to be photographed.

If an outsider had actually seen what Miss Verdier was doing, they would probably have asked themselves why it was that she was taking pictures of those particular nine passengers. What did she find interesting about them? True, they were certainly not as unremarkable as she was, but they didn't really stand out either. She could easily have chosen some other nine. Any nine, actually. The metro is obviously full of such travelers.

But how deceptive appearances can be! If one makes judgments based on external looks and posture, those passengers were certainly not special in any way, but Miss Verdier paid no attention to such things. She did see what is usually unavailable to normal vision, and that was where their interesting qualities were revealed.

Revealed, yes, but not completely at first sight. The first glance was enough to recognize special passengers as such. In order to penetrate their special qualities, however, she had to take their picture. Only in photographs did everything become crystal clear.

Miss Verdier regarded herself as an image interpreter. It was her gift. Others would only see what was shown in a photograph—often not even that—while she saw through into the depths. She saw beyond the visible. She knew how to interpret fully what appeared there. And many things appeared to a gifted eye.

Returning to her seat after she had taken the final, ninth photo, Miss Verdier focused on scrolling through them from the beginning. As the faces appeared one after another on her tablet screen, their names popped, seemingly from nowhere, into her mind: Anatole Mirouille, Marie-Louise Ponthieux, Alain Rigoud, Muriel Julliard, Alexandre Leclair, Maryse Bouvet, Arnaud Morin, Madeleine Prévost, Alfred Leroux-Vidal.

The second round of examination, slower than the first, produced a story for each of the five men and four women: about the perfect clamor for reading, about the return to "Le Boulevard" café after more than half a century, about the beauty of cemeteries, about the encounter between a writer and her characters, about the last selfie, about excessive memories, about the divine sum, about variously colored halos, and about an agent who lost everything.

The third round was the slowest because interpreting was the hardest there. She had to observe a photograph for a long time in order to grasp what was most deeply hidden in it: the dreams of these nine people. If she were to be unsuccessful, she would have no right to consider herself an interpreter. Since she rightly considered herself to be one, the dreams surfaced from the very depths of the pictures. Smiling, she slowly went through them.

$\backsim$ II $\backsim$

IN HIS DREAM, MR. Mirouille went into the bathroom. He didn't usually have any reason to look into the oval mirror above the sink, but this time he stopped in front of it on the way to the shower and stared at his own face. He stood there for a while, when it occurred to him that the most terrible hell would be to live his life over again. It was an unusual thought because he was not a believer who hoped for a continuation of life after death, even one in hell. Besides, he was not of the opinion that his life was so terrible. There were certainly worse ones, if that was any comfort.

Yet he was now horrified by the possibility of repeating it. Next, however, something even darker crossed his mind. What if that repeated life went in the opposite direction—from death toward birth? At first glance that would be desirable: he would become younger and younger, but he would lose the past because he wouldn't remember it. It would turn out that he hadn't lived previously at all. Only an ever briefer future would remain.

Still, that wasn't yet the worst. Right before his own eyes he turned pale when an even stranger chain of events occurred to him. Everything that he had done until now in periods would be unified into a whole in the new life. If he, for example, spent a third of his life sleeping for seven or eight hours per night, in the other life he would sleep for more than two decades without interruption. Other recurring actions would also take place at great length: eating, emptying his bowels and bladder, personal care, working, watching TV, lazing around. . . .

This last idea was the final straw. The other activities, of course, were also unbearable and senseless; but wasting one's time for years doing nothing, that seemed simply inconceivable to him. Even though he had actually loafed around a bit in his life; in short stretches, to be fair, although that was not really a mitigating factor. How many good, useful things he could have done in that time. . .

He shook his head to clear out the disturbing thoughts, then hung up his red terrycloth bathrobe and got into the shower. He reached out to turn on the water, but didn't complete the movement. What if he had died, he suddenly asked himself, and this was already that other life in which everything happened all at once?

He quickly started calculating in his head. He was surprised by the result he got, although it wasn't unexpected. If he spent fifteen minutes a day in the shower, then in his first life he had spent about two hundred and fifty days showering. That meant that, if he were to turn the water on now, the flow wouldn't stop for eight and a half months, and he would be standing there under it all that time.

He broke out in a cold sweat, even though it was warm in the shower. He quickly got out, passed by the mirror without looking, took his bathrobe from the hanger and put it on. Tying the sash around his waist, he stepped out of the bathroom.

∽ III ∾

IN HER DREAM, MISS Ponthieux went into the store. In waking life, it wouldn't even have occurred to her to look in the shop window because the prices would make her head spin, but now she could treat herself. Where else can one act on impulse, if not in one's own dreams? After all, she had good cause. She had decided to kill herself.

She didn't know why, but that wasn't important. Is there anyone who doesn't have a reason to commit suicide? It was far more important to do everything right. Above all, painlessly. That was imperative. She shuddered at pain. There must be a way to leave this world without feeling it. Some sort of pills, for example, which would just make her go to sleep. That would be easiest. She would ask around about that. Anonymously, of course. Over the internet maybe; though she wasn't that good at browsing, she would find a way somehow. Luckily, she was not in a hurry. Once her mind was made up, it made little difference whether she killed herself on this day or that. She could put it off until she was completely satisfied with her preparations.

As for preparations, her first concern was, of course, what she should wear. A man with the same intentions would probably pay little heed to this. He wouldn't care whether he took his own life in his pajamas, his underwear or even completely naked. Yet for a woman, the outfit was crucial. Should she not give special consideration to how she would look on one of the most important days of her life? An occasion no less solemn than a wedding.

Although the event was to be a sad one, black, clearly, was not an option. It would be appropriate if Miss Ponthieux were to attend her own funeral, but she would not, alas, have that opportunity, which was a shame, since she looked really good in black. Something overly cheerful would also not be proper, and especially not white. It was, indeed, to be a solemn event, but after all, it was not a wedding. Although there were women who looked more cheerful on the day of their suicide than on their wedding day.

At the moment she stepped into the store, Miss Ponthieux was certain of only one thing. Whatever the color, the dress for her suicide must be elegant. Fortunately, in her dream the most expensive and thereby the most elegant dresses were available to her. For the first time in her life, she didn't have to worry about expense. Let it cost what it may. She wouldn't even ask the price.

When she was approached by the refined, elegantly dressed saleswoman, Miss Ponthieux was taken aback.

How could she explain what she was looking for? She couldn't ask for a suicide dress. What if they called the police or even the insane asylum? She should have thought of this earlier. An impossible situation, she concluded, wishing to leave without saying a word.

The saleswoman, however, didn't ask her what she wanted. She said nothing. She just took her by the arm and led her to the changing rooms. She pulled back the red plush curtain and indicated what was inside.

"It's already there for you," she said with a smile.

Miss Ponthieux looked at her in puzzlement for a few moments, then went in timidly. She heard the curtain close behind her. The dress was on a hanger. One look convinced her that it was exactly what she wanted. There now, that was the advantage of shopping in fancy stores. They didn't ask you about anything, you didn't have to explain or describe anything. They knew what you were looking for the moment you walked in.

She quickly got changed, then spent some time in front of the mirror looking at herself from all angles. Perfect. She would keep the new dress on, she decided. Why go back to the old one? This was not the day she would kill herself, but what did it matter? One should spend every day as if it is one's last. Now smiling herself, she pulled the curtain back.

◯ IV ◯

IN HIS DREAM, MR. Rigoud found himself in prison. He was sitting on a metal bed, attached to the wall with chains. For bedclothes he had only a threadbare blanket. The olive-drab paint was peeling from the walls. There was no window, just a small opening up near the ceiling. In one corner, a chipped sink, in the other a cracked toilet bowl without a seat. One bare light bulb. Bars on the door, beyond it a dimly lit hallway.

"You know why you're in here," someone said, half-questioningly. Mr. Rigoud stood up from the bed and looked around. He could not determine where the voice was coming from. It seemed to emanate from everywhere.

"I don't know," he answered, looking up because that seemed most appropriate.

"Don't make it harder for yourself, Mr. Rigoud. It's already bad enough. If you cooperate, everything will be less. . . unpleasant."

"I really don't know why I'm in prison. What are you accusing me of?"

"A long indictment could be compiled against you, but we're interested in only one crime. The worst."

"Crime? But I have committed no crime, let alone the worst."

"Really? So, I have to remind you? A pity, we could have skipped this part, but very well, as you wish. Your brother."

Mr. Rigoud's look slid from one corner of the ceiling to the other.

"What about him?"

"He went bankrupt."

"Not my fault."

"Perhaps, but you could have saved him."

"There was no way to save Jacques. He made his own choices."

"It suited you for him to fail. You bought his part of the company for a pittance."

"That was all legal."

"There are laws, and then there are laws. And what about your ex-wife?"

"She has no reason to complain. The divorce made her a wealthy woman."

"It isn't of much use to her in the insane asylum."

"Is it my fault that Annette suffers from hereditary depression? She would have ended up in the nuthouse even if we had stayed married."

"In such a marriage, probably. And then there's your daughter."

"You can't blame me for Sylvie. I paid handsomely to get her off drugs. I did everything I could for her. What can I do if she keeps going back to them?"

"You did everything except be with your daughter while she was getting hooked."

"Her mother was there."

"Who suffers from hereditary depression."

"I can't be expected to do everything. I gave them both a really comfortable life. And that was paid for with time. I had to work long hours."

"And not just work."

Mr. Rigoud looked at the small opening next to the ceiling.

"A man has to live, not just work. Can anyone blame me for that?"

"No, of course not. One must live. And that's actually where the hardest test comes in."

"I don't understand."

"Mr. Rigoud, you are accused of the worst crime a person can commit against themselves. You failed the test of life. You wasted your own life."

This time the silence lasted rather longer.

"So, what now?" the prisoner finally spoke up, more quietly than before.

"Nothing. You are free. You can go back to your wasted life."

Mr. Rigoud turned all around the cell, looked up once more, then headed for the door. It creaked as he opened it.

∽ V ∾

IN HER DREAM, MISS Muriel Juillard settled into the back left-hand seat, and someone quietly closed the door for her. She knew nothing about automobiles, but it was still clear to her that this was a limousine. The interior was all white leather and mahogany; at the wheel was a liveried chauffeur with a cap, separated by a transparent partition.

Next to her was sitting a lady of about forty-five. She was also in a white elegant sleeveless dress, with white elbow-length gloves and a broad-brimmed lemon yellow hat. She was wearing large sunglasses, even though, because of the smoked glass, the back seat was dimly lit.

She waited for the limousine to start moving, almost imperceptibly, before she said anything. She did not turn to face Miss Juillard, but continued looking straight ahead.

"You know that we only have a limited time for this conversation. Use it to the best of your ability. You won't have another chance. Answer briefly and without hesitation. Is all this clear?"

"It is," Miss Juillard quickly answered, nodding.

"All right. What do you want from me?"

"I want you to read my book," she said contritely.

She reached down to take it out of her bag, but the woman in white stopped her with a movement of her finger.

"Why do you want that?"

"Because you are the last reader. No one reads anymore except you. People only write. Everyone is a writer, and there's not a single reader left."

"Too many words. If you also also write like that, that's not good. . . ."

"I don't, I don't. I write quite concisely. Honestly. Here, just look at how thin the book is. . ." Her hand started for her bag again. The finger was even more decisive this time.

"Of all other books, why should I read yours exactly?"

"There is no one else. . . ."

"That certainly isn't reason enough. So a lot of books will go unread, no big deal."

"It's a good book. . . ."

"Good? Now you'll see what's good."

She touched a button on the wide armrest under the window. A partition slid up on the seat in front of her, revealing a shelf full of thick volumes in, inevitably, white bindings.

"Do you know what this is?"

"No," Miss Juillard said, awestruck.

"The cream of the crop. The best of the best. The very pinnacle of world literature. Now, that is good. Tell me, why would your little book be more important than these great works?"

"I'm prepared to pay. . ." the authoress responded hesitantly. Her voice grew quiet. "As much as it takes. . . ."

"As much as it takes?" the lady in white repeated contemptuously. "Aren't you overestimating yourself? Do you have any idea how much? Do you have that much?"

"I do, I do. . . ."

Her hand now moved toward her bag a third time.

This time, however, it was arrested not by a finger but by a shout.

"For God's sake!"

The chauffeur hit the brakes hard, turned around fast and looked sharply at Miss Juillard.

"That's not the way one goes about this," the reader went on in a raised voice. "What do I look like to you? A grocery lady from whom you are buying potatoes, and you want to pay her? Terrible. . ."

"I apologize. . . I. . . didn't mean to. . ."

"No one has ever insulted me like this."

For a while there was silence. The chauffeur kept on frowning at the authoress.

"I think it would be best if I got out. . ." she said.

"And just to think that I was about to make you an offer. . ."

"What?"

"No, no, after this I cannot trust you. You've really disappointed me."

"You can, you can! Believe me! I swear!"

Again they sank into silence. Finally, the woman in white turned her head toward Miss Juillard for the first time.

"I know I'll be sorry for this. Ah, well, here now. I will read your. . . book. Right now, in your presence. While you are still in the car, as we are driving around. It's not too long."

"Really?"

"And it will cost you nothing. I mean, no money, no payment. . ." She looked at the purse in the writer's lap with revulsion.

"I don't know what to say. . . I'm speechless. That's so. . . so nice of you. I would like to pay you back somehow, if there's any way. . . ."

"You can. In the same way."

"What?"

"I must share a secret with you. A big one. You will tell no one, right?"

She darted a glance at the chauffeur. Miss Juillard also looked at him.

"Yes, of course not. Never. Upon my life. You can trust me."

"I'm pleased that you have turned out to be a confidant. Writers must stick together, show solidarity with one another."

"Writers?"

"That's right. I decided to write something myself. It was inevitable. After all these years of reading, I've gathered a wealth of experience that irresistibly desires to be expressed. For money, I read mostly trash, but for my soul I always read the best. The cream of the crop." She pointed with her chin at the white library. "Now I want to make my own contribution to that cream. Can anyone blame me for that?"

"But if you start writing, you will quit reading. Like all the others. Then there will be no one who is reading. . ."

"What can be done? Force majeure. Karma. Anyway, the world won't come to an end if nobody reads."

"Who then will read your work if the whole world stops reading?"

"You."

"I?"

"Yes, of course. As a return favor. I will read your book, and you will read mine. So, what do you say?"

"I. . . This has all taken me by surprise. . . . I would have to think about it. . . ."

"What's there to think about? Your book will be the next-to-last ever read. The last one I will read. Would you have even dared to hope for such an honor? Hand over that book of yours."

Miss Juillard hesitated for only a moment, then, glancing again at the chauffeur, she took the book from her purse. With an expression of disgust, the lady in white pinched it by the corner with two fingers and lowered it onto the armrest.

"All right, but now go ahead and get out. I would rather read alone. I'm more comfortable that way. You will be informed when to come for my book. Until then—mum's the word."

The authoress nodded wordlessly, and at that same moment someone silently opened the door for her.

∽ VI ∾

THE DREAM OF MR. Alexandre Leclair began in front of the confessional. He had never made a confession and he rarely went to church, only when it could not be avoided, for weddings and funerals. He certainly didn't count himself as a believer. Even now he was not sure if he was in the right place, but he had to bare his soul to someone, and a confessor would at least hear him out. He didn't know who else to turn to.

The interior of a confessional he had only seen in films. Perhaps it was not shown properly or he didn't accurately recall, but he was surprised by what he saw when he pushed back the thick dark red curtain. He expected a hassock next to a tiny window in the partition wall, but the stall was filled with a huge armchair, next to which stood a small table with a glass, a flask with some sort of blue liquid, a large crystal ashtray and an illustrated magazine. The armchair was illuminated by a wall-lamp with a green shade.

Mr. Leclair would perhaps have hesitated to go in if he had not been urged on by a melodious female voice on the other side of the diagonally cross-hatched screen on the little window.

"Please, come in, make yourself comfortable."

He sat down hesitantly in the armchair, then tried to see through the screen, but he couldn't make anything out except the hood of a brown cassock.

"Are you comfortable?"

"I think so," he responded after reflecting for a moment.

"We don't have to start right away. Would you like to freshen up first? There is a special energy drink in the flask. Blue Stallion. We produce it ourselves. It's really useful if you're tired, weary, worn out. It brings you back to life. Only figuratively, of course. Everyone knows who alone can really do that."

Mr. Leclair looked at the flask once again. "I'm not thirsty, thank you."

"Perhaps you'd like to smoke? Don't refrain because of those who will come after you. The smoke won't hang around. The ventilation works really well."

"I don't smoke."

"That's smart. There's also a magazine available if you would like to relax a little. The content is secular, even quite explicit. With illustrations. There are no religious articles. We don't want to be accused of canvassing people in trouble."

"I don't care right now about explicit content."

"I understand. Perhaps you would like a neck and shoulder massage? That's the most effective way of getting rid of stress, and there is no one who is not under stress when they come to the confessional. That's the nature of the act."

"A massage?"

"Yes. You decide yourself who will massage you—a male, female or someone in between. They work while we talk. You don't have to worry that they will hear your confession. Some are deaf from birth, and those who aren't listen to loud music through their earphones. They don't have to see you, either. They would wear a blindfold."

"No, thank you, I would rather be alone here."

"Certainly. One more little thing. Does my voice bother you? You can choose another. A male one, let's say, or a child's. . . ."

"A child's?"

"Yes, of course. Whichever. It's important that you can trust it. Many choose their mother's voice for that reason. It's most easy and usual to open your heart to your mother."

Mr. Leclair again fell into brief reflection.

"I didn't confess very often to my mother."

"All right, then we'll go on like this. You haven't made a confession in a long time, have you?"

"A long time," Mr. Leclair responded as if justifying himself. "That's not why I'm here now either."

"Then why?"

"I came here to share my misery. I'm the unluckiest man in the world."

"Don't be so hard on yourself. . . ."

"If only you knew all the misfortunes that have befallen me."

"I'm listening."

Mr. Leclair sighed audibly.

"In a nutshell: first I lost my job; then my wife left me and took the children; my dog broke off his leash during a walk and ended up under the wheels of a car;

my cousin has learned that he's gravely ill; hackers emptied my bank account; and worst of all, I caught my lover with her lover. And all that in just three days." He paused briefly. "You know, I'm not a believer at all, but if I were, I would now lose my faith. How can you believe in a God who is so merciless to you?"

"You're quite wrong. God is more than merciful to you. You are one of his favorites. He adores you. That at least is easily proven."

Mr. Leclair stared for a few moments at the hood on the other side of the screen.

"Easily proven?" he repeated in disbelief.

"Nothing easier, actually. Here, listen. Do you have brothers or sisters?"

"No, I'm an only child."

"Excellent. Is your father still alive?"

"Yes, he is. He's sixty-four."

"Excellent. Did you ever wonder how many sperm there are in an ejaculation?"

Mr. Leclair thought he hadn't heard properly.

"What?"

"It's not unusual if you don't know. Most men have no idea, nor are they particularly interested in it. I will tell you. On average, about five million."

"I knew it was a lot, but I never guessed it was so many. Anyway, what difference does that make?"

"Be patient. Can you guess how many times the average man ejaculates in a lifetime?"

Mr. Leclair tried to figure it out quickly, but wasn't fast enough.

"Don't bother trying. About six thousand times. That means that the average man produces about thirty billion sperm during his life. Someone like your father, for example."

The melodic voice fell silent in order to give Mr. Leclair a chance to respond to this, but he couldn't find the right words, although he wanted to say something.

"Just one of the huge number of your father's sperm fertilized one of your mother's ova. The rest died. The probability that it was precisely that sperm from which you came was, therefore, one in thirty billion. Can you even conceive of how small the chances were?"

Mr. Leclair shook his head, forgetting that he could hardly be seen on the other side of the screen.

"You can't, of course," the confessor went on, as if she had seen him after all. "So, now, essentially it makes no difference if you are a believer or an atheist, if you are one of God's, or chance's, favorites. In both cases, you were enormously, inconceivably lucky. Compared with that, any misfortune that you might face in life is utterly insignificant; least of all the series of unpleasant events that just occurred. That's all irrelevant. It will all pass. Just go on living. That's the only important thing."

Mr. Leclair got up out of the armchair. He felt uncomfortable because he still didn't know what to say.

"You don't have to wait so long to come back again. As you have just seen, we provide consolation for unbelievers as well."

Mr. Leclair's face drew into a smile for the first time. "Good bye," he finally said, and stepped toward the curtain.

∽ VII ∽

IN MRS. MARYSE BOUVET'S dream, she had just passed by a telephone booth when it started ringing. She stopped, thinking that it was strange. She passed this way often, but she had never noticed the booth before. They must have placed it there recently. But why would they do that when they were removing them everywhere else? Who still used phone booths in the era of cell phones? What's more, it was an old-fashioned one. She remembered similar ones from her childhood. She hadn't seen one like it in ages.

The ringing didn't stop. Mrs. Bouvet looked around. There was no one in the vicinity. Maybe she should answer it and tell them they were calling in vain. This was clearly none of her business, but then again, why not show a little courtesy? Maybe it was something important.

When she stepped into the phone booth, the light went on. An unwieldy black telephone with a round dial and a coin slot stood opposite the door, and to the right, on a slightly sloping stand, there was a thick phone book with yellow covers. The door closed softly behind her, muffling the sounds of the outside world. She hesitated for a moment before she picked up the large receiver.

"Hello?"

"Good evening, Mrs. Bouvet," a velvety male voice responded. "Thank you for answering."

She was quiet for a few seconds before speaking again. "This must be some sort of mistake. . . ."

"It's no mistake. You are Mrs. Maryse Bouvet, aren't you?"

"I am, yes, but. . ."

"Then everything is all right. We're looking for you. Welcome to the game show 'My Life'."

Mrs. Bouvet sighed. That's what she got for being courteous. She despised reality shows and now she had stumbled into one against her will. That was the explanation for the old phone booth, and also why the phone had rung just as she was passing. One of those terrible TV channels was behind the whole thing. They were somewhere out of sight, waylaying innocent passers-by. They were recording. They might even be broadcasting live.

She had to hang up and leave immediately. What stopped her, however, was a sudden insight. She was not just an accidental passer-by. If she were, how would they know her name?

"It's not what you're thinking, Mrs. Bouvet," the voice in the receiver went on. "This is definitely no kind of reality show. 'My Life' will not be available to anyone except you. You have my word."

In any other situation, she would have just laughed disdainfully at this, but now she was hindered by the question—how did he know what she was thinking?

"I. . . don't take part in game shows. . ." she said quietly after hesitating a long while.

"I know that. But this is not an ordinary game show. We won't be asking you questions, you will be asking us."

"I'll be asking you? About what?"

"About yourself, of course. In the spirit of the show's name."

"What should I ask you about myself?"

"Anything you want. There are no limits. Then there are the prizes."

"The prizes?"

"Yes, of course. What kind of game show would it be without prizes? Special ones at that. Here at 'My Life' you get a prize whether we know the answers to the questions you ask us or not. If we know, you get one gold coin. If you catch us out—all of five. You can't lose."

"A gold coin?"

"That's right. A real one. Here, like this."

Something rattled through the telephone and fell into the change slot. Mrs. Bouvet carefully stuck two fingers in and pulled out the coin. She held it up to look at it more closely. It really did look golden. True, it could have been a fake, she couldn't tell whether something was real gold or not, but she quashed the doubts inside her. She held on to the gold coin.

"That's payment for agreeing to participate. So, let's get started now. We're waiting for your first question."

Several moments passed while she thought about it.

"How was I dressed the night before last when I went to the movies?"

The velvety voice replied immediately. "A dark blue tweed suit with a light colored blouse. Black shoes with large buckles. Gray overcoat. Matching scarf."

He didn't ask for confirmation that the answer was correct. A new gold coin rattled down into the opening in front of her. She left it there and once again delved into her memory.

"Where did I spend my vacation in 2007?"

The answer again came that very moment: "In Morocco, from August twenty-fifth till September seventh."

She wasn't happy about the new gold coin. Anxiety gripped her. She started to feel somehow exposed, transparent.

"Who was the first person I ever fell in love with?" She asked this more quietly than before. Nobody knew the answer to this. She had never confided in anyone.

"With your French teacher when you were twelve years old."

She completely failed to notice the arrival of the

third gold coin. She had to hold the receiver more tightly so that it wouldn't slip out of her hand, which had suddenly turned damp. This wasn't a game show called "My Life". Who was behind all this? The secret police? Why would they be interested in her? And how could they know about her French teacher? No, something else was afoot. Who knew what? Why, oh why, had she gone into the phone booth? And then allowed herself to be lured by the prizes? With a shaking hand she returned the gold coin in her hand to the change slot.

"I don't want to take part in this anymore," she shouted into the receiver. "You have no right to know everything about my life, about my past. No one has that right. I don't need your gold coins!"

"Life isn't just the past," the velvety voice said gently before she could slam down the receiver and rush out of the phone booth.

"What?"

"You have only one question remaining. Let it be about your future. That's also a part of your life."

This time she went on thinking for a long while, as the unknown caller waited patiently. At first her head was full of questions, but as the minutes went by, they all came down to one. The only one, after all, which remained to be asked about the future.

"How much longer will I live?" she asked finally, her voice flat, as if she was asking something commonplace.

This time the answer did not come from the receiver. To Mrs. Bouvet it seemed that she was no longer in the telephone booth but in a gambling hall, at a slot machine, and that she had just hit the jackpot. From the black box in front of her, gold coins began rattling out.

Soon they filled the change slot, and then they began to spill across the floor of the booth.

"Congratulations, Mrs. Bouvet," the voice came again from the receiver after the golden rain had stopped. "You've won the game show 'My Life'. Spend the gold coins you won wisely. Each of them can last up to a year."

She remained there for a while with the receiver to her ear even after the connection was broken. Then she gently put it down and started gathering the coins. She did not count them. She had no desire to know how many there were. The only important thing was that there were plenty of them. Once they were finally safe in her purse, she left the phone booth smiling.

⌇ VIII ⌇

IN HIS DREAM, MR. Arnaud Morin entered the elevator in the military administration institute where he worked. Two of his uniformed female colleagues were already inside. They were standing in front of a large mirror, their backs to the door. They waited for the doors to start closing behind the newcomer, then turned around.

Mr. Morin looked in surprise at the faces of identical twins. They had barely turned thirty. They were at least a head taller than he, their jackets and skirts closely fitting their curves, with high cheekbones, heavily made up. The one standing on the left was quicker than her colleague: before he could push the button for his floor, she had flipped the switch to halt the elevator.

In the silence which ensued, they looked down at him from above until he began to squirm.

"You know who we are, don't you?" the one on the right finally spoke up.

He hesitated before nodding.

"Who?" asked the one on the left.

"Military intelligence," whispered Mr. Morin.

"Louder!" commanded the one on the right.

Mr. Morin repeated it more loudly, but it was as if he had a lump in his throat.

"You also know why we're here, correct?" the one on the right went on.

This time the hesitation lasted somewhat longer. Still, he didn't wait for them to warn him, but rather hurried to add as loudly as he could: "Because of me?"

"Because of you, of course. But why because of you?"

Mr. Morin glanced first at one beautiful female face, then at the other, then shrugged in resignation.

"You are expected to cooperate, Mr. Morin," the one on the left took over the conversation. "That's the easiest way. Stalling will get you nowhere. It is clear to you that we already know everything, because otherwise why would we be waiting for you in the elevator? So, let's hear it."

"What?" Mr. Morin asked in confusion.

"Don't try my patience," hissed the one on the right.

Again they briefly sank into silence. Then he bowed his head, and once again spoke in a quiet voice. "My hobby?"

The identical beauties looked at each other.

"Hobby?" asked the one on the left.

"Mathematics, numbers, sums. . ." he began to enumerate ruefully.

"Enough of your babbling!" growled the one on the right, her face twisted into an expression of rage. "Take off your clothes!"

He drew back, then asked in disbelief: "I beg your pardon?"

"Or would you rather I undress you? I can do that in an unforgettable fashion."

He glanced at the one on the left as if in supplication. She just nodded her head curtly.

He started gradually to pull off his clothes, laying them on the marble floor of the elevator, but he was hurried along by the angrily tapping foot of the twin on the right. Soon only his underwear was left. He stopped, looking inquiringly at one woman and then the other.

"What are you waiting for?" barked the one on the right.

The one on the left took hold of her arm. "It's enough. For now. Let's hear him out, maybe he's come to his senses."

"Tell me what you want me to admit," whined Mr. Morin. "I'll admit everything."

"Of course you will," said the one on the right, "but not that drivel. Hobby, numbers, mathematics. Nonsense. Who cares about that? You don't really think that we came because of that rubbish?"

"What then?"

"The worst betrayal of all," the one on the left interjected in a soft voice. "The high treason of yourself. You'll admit that you don't know how to live."

He wanted to say something, to object, to offer evidence in his own defense, to justify himself, but he just couldn't find the words.

"You're playing dumb, ostensibly you don't know what we're talking about, right?" asked the one on the right. "Well, now you'll find out. Beyond all doubt. Take a good look at both of us, then say which of us two you would rather make love to."

He stared at the two identical beautiful faces and bodies before him, feeling unbearably awkward. He was supposed to check them out, that's what he'd been ordered to do, but he froze up under their inquisitive, impatient, accusing looks, unable to decide.

"You can't choose?" the one on the right went on. "Then we'll help you a little."

She turned her head toward her sister and smiled; then they also, with synchronized movements, began to remove their clothes. Soon, there were two more piles of clothes on the floor. Only tiny little bras and panties remained on the twins. Black on the left, red on the right.

"And now?" purred the one on the left.

He spoke up only when the one on the right began to hiss like an angry cat.

"Red." It was somewhere between a whisper and a mumble.

A broad smile appeared simultaneously on both women's faces.

"Wrong answer," they said in unison. Then they bent over, picked up their clothes and quickly dressed. As they did so, he stood petrified, not daring to move.

"A man who knows how to live would not have hesitated to choose both," said the one on the left. "Why would he miss such an opportunity?"

"Gather your rags and get out," snapped the one on the right. "You don't even deserve to live."

He was only momentarily tempted to ask for permission to get dressed in the elevator, but he knew he wouldn't get it, so, with head bowed, he picked up his clothes, flipped the switch, waited for the door to open, and went out.

⌒ IX ⌒

MRS. MADELEINE PRÉVOST WAS dreaming that she was on a plane flight. She had just entered the toilet in the tail section. The light grew brighter when she locked the door. She felt tired. She drew close to the mirror and looked at her face. She was pale and had bags under her eyes. She pulled down the skin under her eyes and stuck out her tongue, then shook her head. Why did she even travel when she was in such a state?

She sat on the lid of the toilet which was down, stared into space briefly, then buried her face in her hands. Hardly a moment had passed when a speaker above her began to crackle.

"Lady in the tail section toilet, this is your captain speaking. Are you Madeleine Prévost, the passenger in seat 31F?"

Mrs. Prévost raised her head in confusion. She couldn't precisely determine where the speaker was in the low ceiling.

"Yes."

"Pardon me, but I must ask you what is the purpose of your visit to the toilet? You can talk to me openly, the other passengers cannot hear us."

"What kind of question is that? Why does one go to the toilet anyway?"

"I see that you're not there for the usual reasons."

"You see?" Mrs. Prévost was shocked.

"Yes. You're sitting on the lowered toilet seat and you seem depressed."

She looked quickly all around her, trying to see the camera, but she did not find it.

"It's well hidden, you can't see it."

Mrs. Prévost jumped up from the toilet seat. "How

dare you watch people while they're in the toilet? Why, this is scandalous! Sick voyeurism! I don't want to talk to you anymore. I'll sue your company as soon as we land. This will be all over the news!"

She turned to the door and tried to open it, but without success. She started shaking it, then beat it with her fists. "Open up! Help!" she cried.

"Calm down, Mrs. Prévost. No one can hear you. The door is sound-proofed, and you can't open it by force. You will be released as soon as we establish that you don't have evil intentions."

"Evil intentions?"

"More than ninety-five percent of all hijackings start in the toilet. That is also where they most often put various explosive devices. Whatever you might think of our company, passenger safety is our top priority. What's a little voyeurism, as you call it, if we can save a lot of lives? And trust me, nobody enjoys watching people sitting on the toilet. We are actually like doctors who have to see our patients naked in order to help them. What we see remains completely discreet, and the tapes are erased immediately upon landing."

"You're also recording? This just gets better and better. Alright, will you let me out now? You can see, hopefully, that I don't have evil intentions. I'm not planning to hijack the plane, even less to blow it up, especially since I have no weapons or explosives."

"You never know that."

"How is it not known? I was checked in great detail before getting on the plane."

"You can get hold of explosives after the security check as well."

"And what now? Perhaps you would like to check me out as well. Oh, now I get it. Discreet little doctors want the patient to do a little striptease. Yeah, well, that ain't gonna happen, Biggles. You sorely miscalculated. There will be no nudity for your horny eyes only. If you want to, you can keep me locked up here till we land, but then be ready to suffer the consequences."

"We cannot, unfortunately, keep you locked up till landing. The other passengers also need the toilet."

"So, what will you do then? You don't want to let me out of the toilet, and you don't want to keep me in it. There's no third option."

"There is. A special exit exists for those who are suspected of evil intentions and refuse to cooperate."

Mrs. Prévost once again looked around the small compartment. "I don't see any other exit. Is it also hidden like the camera and speaker, perhaps?"

"It must be."

"And where does it lead? To a jail cell in the cargo hold?" She said this in ridicule.

"No. It leads outside. The floor of the toilet opens up briefly and whoever is inside falls from the plane. Don't count on holding on to something and staying inside. You will simply be sucked out, and at a height of thirty-five thousand feet, the temperature is minus sixty-three degrees Fahrenheit, and the air is quite rarified. In fact there is almost none."

Mrs. Prévost remained speechless for a few moments.

"Why, you're killing passengers," she finally said in a low voice.

"Better for one passenger to die than all of them."

"You're insane. . ." Mrs. Prévost mumbled.

"Sane people facing a very difficult choice."

"All right, you good sane people," she said with a sigh. "If you really want a little striptease so badly that, unless I do it for you, you would throw me out into a vacuum. . . ."

She raised her hand and began to unbutton her blouse.

"A striptease isn't necessary," the pilot stopped her. "There is also a. . . more refined. . . way to determine what your intentions are."

"More refined?"

"Yes. A small test. Every pilot has a different one. One of my colleagues, for example, when they proclaim him—like you did with me a while ago—to be insane, he asks: 'Do you really think I'm crazy?' If the answer is negative, the suspect is thrown out because he was lying just to save himself. If it is positive, he's thrown out because he was right: that's what an insane person would do."

"So, no one survives your colleague."

"Only if they accuse him of being crazy."

"Are you offering me some sort of choice like that?"

"No, nothing of that sort. I would ask you to tell me a story."

"Like Scheherazade?"

"Not really a thousand and one stories. Just one will be enough."

"Any particular one?"

"You choose. The best would be some experience from childhood that has carved itself in your memory. Quite briefly—in just a few sentences."

"And from that you will decide if I am a terrorist?"

"I will. The test works. It's never failed yet."

Mrs. Prévost again mumbled something, this time incomprehensible.

"Beg your pardon?" said the pilot.

"I was wondering—can I think about it for a while?"

"Of course. As long as you like. Keep in mind, however, that I have my finger on the button to open the floor if you try anything. . . ."

"How could I forget that?"

About three minutes later, Mrs. Prévost cleared her throat.

"Here we go. On the way to school I saw two men across the street argue and then start fighting. They really went at each other. Quite soon both their faces were bloody. I got frightened and sped up. Suddenly one of them began to sing. The other guy watched him briefly, confused, and then took up the song. They had really beautiful voices. Their harmonious singing accompanied me all the way to school."

Mrs. Prévost fell silent for a moment, then added: "That's all."

Then she closed her eyes tightly and hugged herself close. A few moments later something clicked. She stood there rigid a while longer, but since there was no whirlwind to suck her out into the frozen airlessness, she opened her eyes and saw that the toilet door was ajar. Without hurrying, she straightened her clothes in front of the mirror and exited.

◌ X ◌

IN HIS DREAM, ALFRED Leroux-Vidal entered the photo booth. He pulled the curtain closed behind him, and sat on the round windup stool. First he examined the camera in front of him. He was surprised when he saw that the opening where the photos came out was inside the booth. This must be a new model, he concluded. Really good. If the opening was outside, someone might be able to get hold of the photos before him. There was one other difference from the older models. The opening wasn't a slot, but a four- or five-inch square. Why did they change that?—he wondered suspiciously.

He didn't need to tidy himself up in the little mirror because his hair was quite short and he was, as on every official occasion, neatly dressed: a dark suit and tie, clean white shirt. He didn't take off his sunglasses. He tried several expressions. All were seriously grim or grimly serious. He didn't smile even once. A smile just didn't go with his face.

He froze and then pushed the button. He was expecting a flash, but there was none. Apparently there was enough light in the booth. Just as he was thinking that, something rattled in the machine, and a small object fell into the opening. He recognized that it was a pacifier only on second glance. First he just looked at it a bit, not touching it, then he cautiously picked it up and gave it a sniff. He twirled it briefly between his fingers. Finally, he pushed his knees together and put it in his lap.

He pushed the button again, curious as to what would happen next. He didn't freeze because even without doing so he seemed stiff enough. The rattle this time was even louder. The explanation for the clanging sound appeared in the form of a small blue metal automobile. He no longer had to hesitate, but his professional caution drove him to look at it more carefully for a while before he picked it up. How much time had passed since the last time he had held it? A good forty years.

He put it next to the pacifier, then pushed the picture button one more time. It was silly to call it that, in fact, when there was no picture-taking. As the third object came down, he could tell by the sound that it would be something heavier with soft edges, but a tennis ball never crossed his mind. He didn't hesitate to pick it straight up. He turned it over and saw the now fading signature of the greatest tennis player of that time. For a moment he was once again filled with his old admiration as he placed the ball in his lap.

No longer looking into the lens, he again pushed the button which in some magical way was returning to him loved objects from his past. Into the opening this time came a gray thumb-drive. This made him really happy. He was convinced that he had long, long since lost it. That he would never again see the photos which had only been saved onto it. Photos from that summer in the mountains when so many things happened to him for the first time. Fearing that he might lose it again, he wanted to put it immediately in one of his many inside pockets, but that wouldn't be fair toward the other precious things, so it ended up in his lap, too. It would be safe there.

His medal arrived fifth. The only one he had ever gotten. Secretly. In his profession, commendations were handed out without witnesses or celebrations. You hold the medal for a few minutes, as long as the ceremony lasts, then you hand it over to the service for preservation. After fifty years, if you're still alive, you have a chance to see it again in the service museum. Not even then is your name attached to it. They only say why it was given, but not to whom. Usually medals are given for taking life. Only rarely for saving it. Mr. Leroux-Vidal was very proud of the fact that his belonged to the second category, although that would never be known outside of a very small circle of the informed few.

A key came sixth. It opened the front door of the little house in the village, the only place where he could pretend to be an ordinary citizen. Quite rarely and quite briefly. Not more than two or three weekends a year. Even then he didn't dare to see anyone, to be in anyone's company, to be on the phone with anyone or have any other relationships. He could just isolate himself, read, watch TV or do whatever it is that those without company do. And certainly not start thinking about whether he was satisfied with his life. Or what the meaning of life is at all.

A pine cone surfaced from the opening seventh. It had fallen between two graves at the small cemetery in the provinces. Something closer to the headstone on which stood only initials, from which no one would ever conclude that here, in fact, Mr. Leroux-Vidal lay at rest.

Now, in his dream, before he ended up under that headstone, he reached out toward the machine to push for the eighth time the button which took no pictures, but he never completed the action. What else could appear in the square opening after the pine cone? He cupped his hands and picked up the seven objects in his lap, stood up, moved the little curtain back with his elbow, and went out.

∽ XI ∾

ONCE SHE HAD PENETRATED into the ninth dream as well, Miss Verdier sighed with relief, laid the tablet in her lap and looked up. She was not surprised when she saw that there was no one else in the carriage any-more. Actually, it was no longer even the same carriage. While it remained unchanged on the side where she was sitting, it was now completely different on the other. The windows had disappeared, along with the seats and the three sliding doors, and instead some other openings and doors had appeared: a bathroom door, a curtain for a changing room, bars on a jail cell, a car door, the curtain of a confessional, the door of a phone booth, an elevator door, the door of an airplane toilet, the curtain on a photo booth.

Miss Verdier smiled in order to greet graciously the visitors who were just about to arrive from their dreams. And indeed, all nine appeared at the same moment, as if they had arranged it: Mr. Anatole Mirouille in his terrycloth robe, Miss Marie-Louise Ponthieux in her elegant dress, Mr. Alain Rigoud in his pinstriped suit, Miss Muriel Juillard full of writer's aspiration, Mr. Alexandre Leclair stunned by the enormous numbers, Mrs. Maryse Bouvet and her purse heavy with gold coins, Mr. Arnaud Morin just in his underwear with a pile of clothes in his hands, Mrs. Madeleine Prévost with her recently acquired fear of flying, and Mr. Alfred Leroux-Vidal and his bunch of little objects.

The visitors stood for just a moment, confused, at the nine entrances to the carriage. Then they quickly realized where they were, and immediately everything was clear to them. They themselves smiling, they headed toward Miss Verdier, who obviously could no longer be overlooked.

Contributors

About the author

Zoran Živković was born in Belgrade, Serbia, on October 5, 1948. Until his recent retirement, he was a full professor at the Faculty of Philology, the University of Belgrade, teaching creative writing. He is one of the most translated contemporary Serbian writers: by the end of 2017 there were 93 foreign editions of his books of fiction, published in 23 countries, in 20 languages.

Živković has won several literary awards for his fiction, beginning with the Miloš Crnjanski award in 1994 for his novel *The Fourth Circle*. In 2003, Živković's mosaic novel *The Library* won a World Fantasy Award for Best Novella; in 2007 his novel *The Bridge* won the Isidora Sekulić award; and in 2007 he received the Stefan Mitrov Ljubiša award for lifetime achievement in literature. In 2014 and 2015 he received three awards for his contribution to the literature of fantastika: Art-Anima, Stanislav Lem and The Golden Dragon.

Zoran Živković has been recognized with his selection as European Grand Master for 2017 by the European Science Fiction Society at the 39th Eurocon in Dortmund, Germany.

Živković is the author of 22 books of fiction:
   The Fourth Circle (1993)
   Time Gifts (1997)
   The Writer (1998)
   The Book (1999)
   Impossible Encounters (2000)
   Seven Touches of Music (2001)
   The Library (2002)
   Steps through the Mist (2003)
   Hidden Camera (2003)
   Compartments (2004)
   Four Stories till the End (2004)
   Twelve Collections and the Teashop (2005)
   The Bridge (2006)
   Miss Tamara, The Reader (2006),
   Amarcord (2007)
   The Last Book (2007)
   Escher's Loops (2008)
   The Ghostwriter (2009)
   The Five Wonders of the Danube (2011)
   The Grand Manuscript (2012)
   The Compendium of the Dead (2015)
   The Image Interpreter (2016)

About the artist

Youchan Ito was born 1968 in Aichi prefecture, Japan. She launched her career as a graphic designer in 1988, becoming a freelancer illustrator in 1991 and founding Togoru Co., Ltd. with her husband in 2000. In 2017 the company was reborn as Togoru Art Works. She works with a wide range of genres including cover art and design for science fiction, mysteries and horror titles, as well as illustrations for children's books.

www.youchan.com